Kissing Ellie was like finding harbour after an endles **sex and lust th any normal wo to begin with But then her hands went round his neck and she dragged him close. Her abandon startled him, delighted him. But it was also his cue to back right off. Hadn't the past taught him anything?**

Turning his face away from her, he wiped his mouth with the back of his hand. He was almost desperate to eradicate the taste of her. He doubted he'd ever succeed. She'd tasted fresh and young and eager and innocent. And he wanted her.

'Is that supposed to keep me quiet?' she asked him, with contempt in her voice.

He looked at her. She was shaking, but not from fear.

'This is going nowhere—'

'You think I'd want it to?' she asked incredulously, while her body told him something else.

He watched her stalk away with a heady mix of lust and relief. That was Ellie Mendoras over and done with. His attention was needed elsewhere. Business called, and in his world business always came first.

Susan Stephens was a professional singer before meeting her husband on the tiny Mediterranean island of Malta. In true Modern™ style they met on Monday, became engaged on Friday and were married three months after that. Almost thirty years and three children later, they are still in love. (Susan does not advise her children to return home one day with a similar story, as she may not take the news with the same fortitude as her own mother!)

Susan had written several non-fiction books when fate took a hand. At a charity costume ball there was an after-dinner auction. One of the lots, 'Spend a Day with an Author', had been donated by Mills & Boon author Penny Jordan. Susan's husband bought this lot, and Penny was to become not just a great friend but a wonderful mentor, who encouraged Susan to write romance.

Susan loves her family, her pets, her friends and her writing. She enjoys entertaining, travel and going to the theatre. She reads, cooks, and plays the piano to relax, and can occasionally be found throwing herself off mountains on a pair of skis or galloping through the countryside. Visit Susan's website: www.susanstephens.net—she loves to hear from her readers all around the world!

BOUGHT:
ONE ISLAND,
ONE BRIDE

BY
SUSAN STEPHENS

◎™ MILLS & BOON®
Pure reading pleasure

All the characters in this book have no existence outside the imagination
of the author, and have no relation whatsoever to anyone bearing the
same name or names. They are not even distantly inspired by any
individual known or unknown to the author, and all the incidents are
pure invention.

First published in Great Britain 2007
Harlequin Mills & Boon Limited,
Eton House, 18-24 Paradise Road, Richmond, Surrey TW9 1SR

© Susan Stephens 2007

ISBN: 978 0 263 85376 6

Set in Times Roman 10½ on 12¾ pt
01-1207-51291

Printed and bound in Spain
by Litografia Rosés, S.A., Barcelona

BOUGHT:
ONE ISLAND,
ONE BRIDE

For Jenny, and The Team

CHAPTER ONE

THE only time he relaxed was when he was here on the island of Lefkis, but today was different…

Alexander Kosta, saviour of the island? The mayor speaking to the crowd was calling him that. It was better that than the truth, Alexander supposed. A ruthless tycoon who had identified an opportunity didn't have quite the same ring to it.

His gaze strayed beyond the canvas-draped pavilion to the clear blue ocean beyond the harbour. He noted how the sea turned broody and emerald in the distance, and how the sugared-almond-coloured houses clustered round the perfect horseshoe bay had turned more vivid in the late-afternoon sunshine. The island of Lefkis was beautiful and unspoiled, and when it was put up for sale he had been ready.

He noticed everything, and today a young woman had distracted him. Standing in the prow of an old fishing boat, the only flaw in an otherwise picture-perfect panorama, she was glaring at him. He had given instructions for the harbour to be cleared of craft with shallow draft to make way for the super-yachts, but she was still there.

Ellie Foster, or Ellie Mendoras, as she called herself to honour her dead Greek father, had been chosen by the islanders to voice their objections to his vision of progress for

Lefkis. But she didn't know the history behind his purchase, and she clearly didn't know what she was up against.

Perhaps he should be glad she had remained on her boat. The crowd was quiet, but if she joined them that would change. Charm was his weapon of choice in a situation like this, and he knew the dissenters would come round. The wealth he could bring to their island was irresistible.

He looked at the girl again. Her very presence was an insult. Dressed drably in what appeared to be a boiler suit, she couldn't have drawn a sharper contrast to the glamour girls surrounding him. And could her scowl possibly deepen?

Everyone else was smiling at him... Everyone smiled at him all the time, now he came to think about it. Why wouldn't they? The charisma of massive wealth worked its magic everywhere he went. Alexander Kosta was the success story everyone wanted a piece of. Born in a shack, he had learned at an early age that the only certainty in life was the food *he* put on the table, and the only love he could count on was the love that could be bought.

He could buy anything he wanted now, including an island. He had added Lefkis to his property portfolio as he might have added a vase he coveted from the estate of a man who in life had been both his greatest enemy and the greatest spur to his ambition. He envisaged a mini-Dubai springing up where once there had been bare rock and poverty. It was a wonder the island had survived beneath the heel of his predecessor, Demetrios Lindos.

The girl should thank him, Alexander thought, glancing at Ellie. The power-boat race was just the start of the improvements he intended to make. There would be hotels, luxury spas, shopping malls... Everyone would benefit, including the troublemaker on her old fishing boat.

Hearing a few locals murmur against his scheme, Alexander firmed his jaw. If they couldn't see what he was trying to do— *if she stopped them seeing what he was trying to do…*

She was preparing to disembark. Although she was too far away for him to see her features clearly, the tilt of her chin told a story of its own. Did she really intend to confront him? She had some nerve. The world measured him by what he owned and what he could buy, and everyone listened when he spoke. She should be down on her knees rejoicing that he had arrived in time to save her tinpot island.

Alexander watched Ellie stride determinedly towards him down the quay. Her God-given certainty that she was on the side of the angels got right under his skin.

As if reading his mind, the crowd turned to look in the same direction. He could feel the tension rising as though everyone sensed a storm brewing. They settled again, reluctantly, and stared at him. They weren't sure what to do. They'd had a taste of his generosity in the free food and entertainment he'd provided, and wanted more. In spite of the girl's determination to disrupt the proceedings he judged them more than ready to listen to his plan.

She was nothing to him; a nobody. He shut her out. The crowd was warming to him. Sunlight bathed the scene, enhancing the colours of the bunting fluttering over his head. The wind had dropped, turning the ocean into a limpid lake. This was his island. This peaceful and lovely scene belonged to him now. Ellie Mendoras had made her first big mistake, because if she was looking for trouble, she'd found it.

Money-making was Alexander Kosta's greatest skill in life. His only skill in life, Ellie told herself contemptuously as she marched down the quay. In spite of everything he had achieved, he wasn't satisfied. He was still hungry for conquests, still searching for the next challenge; the next acquisition.

Well, he could keep his greedy hands off Lefkis. She had vowed to uproot and dislodge him before the tentacles of his empire had the chance to squeeze the life out of the island she loved.

But even as Ellie narrowed her eyes and dreamed of bringing the Greek tycoon to his knees, her heart rebelled and thundered a warning. She wasn't brave. She had never put her head above the parapet before. She lived quietly on the island she loved, surrounded by the gentle people who had helped her heal after a terrible experience back in England had nearly destroyed her.

Which was precisely why she had to help those people now, Ellie determined, quickening her step. Maybe the islanders had mistaken her for her father, Iannis Mendoras, a true hero, but she wouldn't let them down. Walking in the footsteps of a giant was impossible, but she wouldn't disgrace her father's name.

Alexander Kosta had drawn quite a crowd. The market square was packed, with visitors and with locals. She could see him clearly now.

And he took her breath away, Ellie admitted reluctantly. Her heart was throbbing at a ridiculous pace—and it wasn't just Alexander's good looks that had thrown her, but the power he exuded. She told herself that no one could have been prepared for that.

Ellie shied away from men after her experience back in England, and this Alexander Kosta was brazenly male. But now the locals were clustering at her elbows, urging her on. They depended on her and she couldn't turn her back on them now…

Alexander's face hardened as he finished his speech and the women, or birds of paradise, as he thought of them, clustered around him. The girls' silk dresses fluttered in the breeze, raising a haze of exotic scent. His fabulous yacht, the *Olympus*, had brought out every woman of marriageable age irrespective of the fact that she might already be attached to some dupe who had been taken in by her porcelain smile and artificially inflated chest. He took a perverse pleasure in the games the birds of paradise played, but most of all he liked to see them falter when they realised how deeply he despised them.

As the crowd erupted into applause he shrugged the women off. He didn't want their air kisses. He was more interested in glancing in triumph at the cliff-top where Demetrios Lindos's grand old house was being demolished stone by stone. He would rebuild the house where his young wife had sold her body to an old man, but before he did that he would raze it to the ground and stand amongst the ashes.

He was forced to pause as Ellie Mendoras joined the crowd and the voices of protest rose against him again. He understood the reason for it, though that didn't excuse her. Demetrios Lindos had been a harsh tyrant who had kept the island poor, and some of the locals feared he might be worse. It was that fear talking now. But it wouldn't weaken his resolve; the improvements he intended to bring to the island would be made.

Alexander glanced at the old fishing boat. It jarred on him more than the discontent in the crowd. She had inherited the boat from her Greek father, and according to his sources had painstakingly converted it to accommodate tourists on her watered-down lecture tours. She could conduct those tours perfectly well from the new berth he had offered her. She wouldn't be allowed to take up one of the precious deep-water berths when they were all spoken for.

He would crush her rebellion before it spread like an infection, Alexander determined, watching Ellie. Some might think this too small a problem for him to be concerned with, and that trouble was something a man like Alexander Kosta encountered on a world stage, but experience had taught him that a small problem like this spat with a local girl could grow out of all proportion if he ignored it.

She had reached the back of the crowd, from where her eyes blazed defiance at him. Ellie Mendoras, environmental warrior, versus Alexander Kosta? His lips quirked in amusement. Confrontation turned him on. As far as Ellie Mendoras was concerned the situation between them was black and white; he was the enemy, while she was the true saviour of her people. For him the situation held a far more interesting range of possibilities.

As she drew closer his hackles rose. He had declared today a holiday and most people had taken the trouble to dress up. Ellie Mendoras was still in her work clothes, and, apart from sun-bleached auburn hair hanging almost to her waist, she might have been taken for a boy. All that prevented her from appearing completely sexless was the beguiling fire in her eyes, and that was all directed at him.

He watched as she tried and failed to fight her way through the crowd. There was a group of his hard-core supporters at the front. Her face had set in a tight mask of disapproval. Her army had deserted her. Most people were intrigued by his vision of the future. Why couldn't she get it through her head that his way was the only possibility of bringing wealth to Lefkis?

Flexing his muscular frame with impatience, Alexander ordered himself to forget Ellie Mendoras. For a man who had risked much to achieve more, a girl like that shouldn't even register on his radar. Firing one last glance at the small, determined figure straining to see over the shoulders of the crowd, he shut her out completely.

* * *

Frustration had tightened a band of steel around her chest. There were so many visitors standing at the front, none of whom, judging by their expensive clothes, had anything to lose by sucking up to Alexander Kosta. The locals were in danger of being ignored if she didn't make her move soon. She had to find a way to reach the stage and snatch the microphone out of Alexander Kosta's hand. She had to make sure the locals' cause was voiced.

Adrenalin was racing, prompting her to act, but the podium was guarded by security staff...

She had to wait. She had to move slowly closer and remember what was at stake. The glamorous folk she was standing with now had no interest in local culture. Their goal was to line their pockets at the locals' expense. They would suck the island dry and then move on to the next novelty destination. She had to make them see sense. She had to make the man behind this monstrous plan see sense...

Ellie paused to compose herself when she reached the side of the platform. Alexander Kosta, a man in his mid-thirties, was commanding the stage. His charisma alone could hold an audience in awe. What chance did she stand against him?

Whispers from unseen faces urged her forward. That was all she needed to hear. The locals needed her. They were frightened of Alexander Kosta, and were begging her to speak for them.

She was frightened too, Ellie admitted to herself. Beneath his easy smile and handsome face she sensed the ice in Alexander Kosta. This was not a man to cross. This was not a man to take on. He might have been granted the blazing good looks of a film star, but he was not play-acting. She guessed the lightweight linen suit had been precision-tailored to fit his muscular frame, and beneath the open buttons at the neck of his crisp white shirt she could see a lot more than she cared to of the hard, tanned body underneath.

She flinched as he caught her staring. The fact that he had noticed her at all should have acted as a warning, and, to make it worse, her pulse was roaring. She was thankful when he turned his head away as if to say she was of no consequence to him.

But then Ellie realised to her astonishment that she wanted Alexander Kosta to look at her; she *wanted* him to notice her. It was hard to break the fascination with his piercing sea-green gaze and black, stubble-shaded jaw. His sensual lips and cold expression were so at odds with each other, and there was an erotic haze around him that both frightened and intrigued her. But she had to act, since no one else was prepared to. His intention to bring power-boat racing to the seas of Lefkis was moving forward like a juggernaut that no one could stop. The crowd was hypnotised by his almost mythical status, but a change of thinking could be brought about by a single voice, and today that voice would be heard.

'Go on, Ellie…'

Murmurs were rising all around her, and she was on the point of making her move when the audience applauded and Kosta smiled. As he raked a hand through his hair he seemed almost boyish… But she knew he was a ruthless tycoon—she couldn't be fooled.

Launching herself forward, she mounted the stage. As she tore across the platform Alexander Kosta started moving towards her. The reflexes of his trained men were no match for his speed…

She froze halfway. And then there was chaos. Women screamed and milled about, while Kosta's bodyguards were caught up in the mêlée.

'Don't touch me! Don't you dare touch me!' Ellie shouted, backing away. The look in Alexander's eyes terrified her. She was panicked by his overwhelming maleness.

'Not so brave now, are you?' he observed with satisfaction.

'What good are your bodyguards to you?' she scoffed, rallying to make her stand.

'What do you want?' he demanded harshly.

'Nothing more than a fair hearing—'

'And is this how you go about it?'

'How else am I supposed to make you listen?' Ellie was aware her voice was rising. 'Will you hear me out?'

'Now?'

She stood her ground. 'I can think of no better time.'

'What do you think you have achieved by this?' He threw an angry glance over his shoulder, and then turned back to her.

What had happened to all the things she had planned to say? She should be railing at him, but instead awareness was shimmering through her. Her senses were heightened from fear, and from exertion, Ellie reasoned, and because of that adrenalin was racing through her system. And if Alexander Kosta would just look away for a single moment she would compose herself...

But he didn't look away.

'Explain yourself,' he ordered coldly.

'I'm speaking for the people of Lefkis—'

'Your people?'

The sneer in his voice was all it took to trip the detonator in her mind. 'You care nothing for them,' she declared passionately, when she had vowed to be cool and reasoned. 'You're just like all the other oligarchs who visit Lefkis in their white water-borne caravans—'

'For someone who wasn't even born on the island, you have a lot to say for yourself,' Alexander Kosta observed coolly.

'My father was born here. He was—'

'A fisherman? Yes, I know. And your mother was an English woman who deserted him.'

'It wasn't like that...' Ellie knew she was losing control when it was imperative to remain clear-headed. But when Kosta dared to criticise her family— 'My mother made a choice, and I respect that—'

'Respect?' One brow shot up.

'My English mother taught me respect,' Ellie returned coldly, 'which is why I honour my Greek father's name—'

'And why the locals have asked you to speak for them? From what I know, your mother chose safe suburbia over her Greek lover, and you didn't so much as set foot on this island until she died—'

The callous way in which he was talking about the parents she loved fuelled Ellie's anger. 'When I came here I fell in love with the island and its people.' One part of her brain simply refused to accept that she had also been running as fast as she could from an elderly friend of her mother's who had attacked her when her guard was down.

He had to court this woman. He couldn't cast her aside, though he sincerely wished he could. The locals trusted her; loved her, even. She was the key to unlock this island and make his vision of progress run smoothly. When her father had been lost at sea the locals had adopted her. On that day Ellie Mendoras hadn't become the orphan she had expected to be, but the cherished daughter of a family in mourning; a family that encompassed every living soul on Lefkis. The hold she had over them was his last remaining sticking point. 'You don't belong here!' he exploded, uncharacteristically losing his cool even after reasoning things through. 'You're not even Greek.'

'My heart belongs here!' she roared back at him.

She roared at him? Was Alexander Kosta losing his fabled self-control? It was time to put things back on an even keel. 'Lefkis belongs to me now,' he reminded her, with a closing gesture of his hands.

'You don't frighten me!'

Didn't she know when to be quiet? 'Really?' he said with menace. 'Then perhaps I should.'

A shiver tracked down Ellie's spine as she gazed up at Alexander. She'd had no idea they would engage in a fight like this. She had imagined his bodyguards would cart her off, once she'd had her say, which would be long past by now. But there was a passion between them, the air simmered with tension. Ellie stood her guard, held her head high; she knew Kosta didn't so much as pay lip-service to the meek and mild. His goal was clear, and he was determined to drive it through.

But so was she. 'We survived the rule of Demetrios Lindos, and we will defeat you—'

'Brave words, Ellie Mendoras, but where is your army now?' He glanced around. The audience was waiting patiently for him to return. 'It looks to me like these people don't want to be stuck in the past with you and Demetrios Lindos, after all.'

Ellie flushed red. Where the past was concerned Kosta was right—a part of her would always be locked there.

'Why do you stay on the island?' he probed. 'What is it to you?'

My sanctuary, Ellie thought immediately, but no way would she tell him that. She sought safety in the facts instead. 'Lefkis was my father's home, and now it is mine—'

'Then if you wish to remain here, you had better learn to accept change like everyone else.'

That was a threat, Ellie realised, but she had gone too far to crawl back. 'Change prescribed by you?'

'That's right, Ms Mendoras.'

Of course. The man who had bought the island could do anything he wanted to. And she had felt so safe here at one time, Ellie thought wistfully, but now there were so many strangers on the island; people she didn't know, men she didn't know—

'I don't have time for this,' he said.

She jerked away.

'I have no intention of touching you, Ms Mendoras.'

Why was she so frightened of him? Alexander asked himself. It was then he noticed the scar. Round and ugly on her cheek, it looked as though someone had tried to put their brand on her. And when she saw him staring at it she brought her hair down, using her fingers like a comb to cover it.

He switched his attention. He had no intention of making any of this personal. 'See to the ladies,' he commanded to the bodyguard who had approached. He threw a contemptuous glance at the squawking females, some of whom were still milling about the stage.

Ellie tried to moisten her lips with a tongue turned suddenly dry. She was surrounded by powerful men, but Alexander Kosta had no need of bodyguards when he could hold her in place with nothing more than a stare. She watched the women on the platform being ushered down the steps like so many sheep. Panic had made them shrill and their bird-like voices grated on her. Shouldn't they also reassure her? Ellie reasoned. Alexander Kosta would hardly be interested in molesting her when he'd brought his harem.

Ellie had to stop herself tracing the scar on her cheek. She had no doubt Kosta had not only noticed, but had also calculated how she got it. She felt vulnerable. She didn't want him to know anything about her. She had to be strong and not allow herself to be distracted.

But that scar was a mark of her past... The worst of it was, she had trusted and admired the old man who had attacked her. He had been a friend of her late mother's, and had been kind to her. He had been one of the first to offer friendship when her mother died. She just hadn't realised how many strings were attached to that friendship. He was the reason she had fled to Lefkis and, though he was nothing like Alexander Kosta, he had left her with a fear of men that had never faded.

'So, Ms Mendoras...'

Ellie looked at Alexander.

'What am I going to do with you?'

Everything had quietened on stage and they were alone on the platform. The physicality of the man facing her, his sheer brute strength... 'How do you know so much about me?'

As his sensual lips curved in a confident smile she noticed that his eyes remained cold.

'I make it my business to know everything that happens on this island.'

'Then you must know my determination—'

'To speak? Yes, I do,' he said as if this was obvious. 'But not here and not today.' And when she started again he added firmly, 'This is not the appropriate forum for a heated discussion, Ms Mendoras—'

'So you say—'

'Yes, I do say.'

To her amazement he flicked out a business card. 'I think you'll find there are better ways of getting your point across.' His voice turned faintly mocking. 'For example, you could make an appointment with my secretary...'

She had massively underestimated him. She had pictured

herself in the middle of an impassioned protest that included all the locals. But where were they? Had Kosta won them over with little more than a fairground for the children, and an endless supply of good food and wine…?

As a member of his security team approached them Ellie guessed this was the moment when she would be bundled unceremoniously off the stage.

The man glanced at her as he whispered something to his master, and Kosta smiled and shook his head. Then he added some remark in Greek she couldn't catch. 'This isn't funny, Kirie Kosta—'

'Am I laughing, Ms Mendoras?' he snapped icily. 'May I remind you that I have a speech to complete when I have finished with you?'

The crowd had waited a long time for him to return, and still they were quiet. They were satisfied he had everything in hand and had forgotten her, Ellie realised.

'Shall I ask my PA to expect your call?' Kosta prompted.

'You'd meet with me?'

'It's that simple, Ms Mendoras.'

His husky tone strummed an unwelcome chord inside her, which Ellie tried very hard to ignore.

'There's really no need for all this drama…'

Ellie squeezed her eyes shut briefly in defeat. But wasn't this everything she wanted? Alexander Kosta offering to meet with her? The faint spice of his cologne invaded her nostrils, reminding her how closely they were standing.

'Take my offer,' he said coldly, 'or leave it. I really don't care.'

Ellie's gaze rested on the business card. 'I'm not agreeing to anything until you allow me speak to the crowd—'

'Why would they want to listen to you? What could you possibly offer them?'

He was right, Ellie realised with frustration. 'If no one cares about Lefkis, as you suggest, what is the point in my making an appointment to see you?'

'Because *you* care?' he challenged. 'Now, are we finished, Ms Mendoras?'

Ellie's anger grew as she remembered the eviction notice that had been served on her that morning. All the other fishermen had left the deep-water harbour, but she had stayed on because they had asked her to make this protest. She could see how naïve she'd been now. 'Yes, we're finished. I have wasted enough time on a man who doesn't care about this island or its people—'

'You make a lot of assumptions about me. And if you won't stop this nonsense now I think we'd better talk sooner rather than later.'

Ellie's throat constricted with panic as Alexander beckoned to one of his men. Her flesh crawled at the thought of some man she didn't know touching her.

'Escort this young lady to the *Olympus*. I'll deal with her when I've finished here. Ms Mendoras will be my guest,' he added, as an afterthought.

The man's attitude towards her changed immediately. His boss's message to treat her with respect had been received.

'I'm not going anywhere,' Ellie said stubbornly.

She was looking at his yacht and he could see the fear in her eyes. Good. Girls like Ellie Mendoras should be taught a lesson. A yacht the size of the *Olympus* wasn't just another boat in the harbour, it was another country, subject to its own rules and boundaries, all of which were decided by him. She knew that once on board she would be cut off from the outside world.

'I prefer neutral ground,' she insisted.

'I'm afraid you have no choice in the matter.' He nodded to his man.

He felt his senses stir. The chase excited him. He would close her down and end the protest very soon.

'I couldn't…be alone with you,' she said hesitantly.

The protest was over that easily? Surely not! 'I'm sure I can answer your concerns.' He gave a curt nod, telling his man to keep an eye on her.

A rousing cheer greeted him as he returned to the stage. He had to wait for the crowd to quieten down before he could speak. When they did he asked them to be patient a little longer, and, leaning from the stage, he identified a local woman who he knew commanded respect, and asked her to join him.

Ellie couldn't hide her surprise when Alexander came back with Kiria Theodopulos. The old lady was one of the elders of the island, and highly respected. 'What are you doing?' she asked him suspiciously.

'Since you feel the need for a chaperon, I have invited Kiria Theodopulos to join us on my yacht.'

Ellie shivered inwardly. Alexander Kosta was blocking her every move, but she couldn't waste this opportunity to put the locals' case for purely selfish reasons. 'All right,' she agreed, 'I'll do it.'

CHAPTER TWO

'YOU are well-meaning, but misguided, Ms Mendoras.'

'And you are an arrogant plutocrat who presumes he knows what's best for everyone…'

OK, this was not going exactly to plan. The atmosphere between them was deteriorating rapidly. It seemed they couldn't inhabit the same space without passions being roused.

Ellie and Alexander were confronting each other in Alexander's study on board the *Olympus*. She was standing stiff and angry on one side of his desk, while Alexander lounged comfortably in a padded leather chair on the other.

As far as he was concerned he alone knew what was best for the island, Ellie fumed. He wasn't prepared to listen to anyone else's point of view, least of all hers. Just as she had imagined, the *Olympus* was more than a floating home; the yacht was Alexander Kosta's kingdom—a kingdom he ruled without a council.

'Why don't you sit down and relax, Ms Mendoras?'

He pointed to the comfortable chair one of his lackeys had drawn up for her.

'I'm here to make a point, not to make myself comfortable.'

'Please yourself.' He shrugged.

Ellie was deeply conscious that, sitting silently some distance away from them, Kiria Theodopulos was a party to everything. The old lady was both her rock and her sticking point. She felt safe, but she couldn't say half the things she would have liked to. Respect for the old lady's traditional values meant she had to keep a curb on her tongue. 'Mr Kosta—'

'Ms Mendoras? Or may I call you Ellie?'

As Kiria Theodopulos gave an almost imperceptible nod Ellie knew she didn't have much alternative.

'Good,' he said smoothly, 'and in that case I have no objection to you calling me Alexander...'

'You're too kind.' She could think of plenty more things she'd like to call him, but for now *Alexander* would have to do.

'So, tell me what's on your mind,' he prompted.

In truth? Very little right now. Ellie's mind had emptied faster than a sieve. Calling Alexander Kosta by his first name was far too intimate for her liking. But she could handle it, Ellie reassured herself. 'You can't expect to throw Lefkis open to all comers, Alexander, and have no consequences...'

He took his time to answer her and rubbed one firm thumb pad across the stubble on his chin before he did.

'You seem to know a lot about my future plans for the island, Ellie.'

His expression suggested quite the contrary; that she knew nothing.

'Do you really care for this island, or was your protest today prompted by self-interest?'

'What?' Ellie couldn't believe her ears.

'It just seems to me to be too much of a coincidence that on the day you learn you are about to lose your berth in the deep-water harbour you launch a campaign against me...'

Kiria Theodopulos stiffened as if she would have liked to intervene. 'Of course I care about my berth,' Ellie said quickly, wanting to save the old lady further hurt. 'It was my father's, and his father's before him.' Her eyes turned to emerald ice as she held Alexander's gaze, daring him to contradict her.

'Well, I just can't understand your concerns. What is wrong with your new berth on the other side of the island?'

'Exactly my point!' Ellie blazed. 'It's on the other side of the island. Why is that, Alexander? Is the fishing fleet too unsightly for your new visitors? Will everyone who fails to live up to your exacting standards be replaced or relocated where they can't be seen? What will you do if your wealthy friends complain about the lack of local colour? Will you have us bussed in?'

Kiria Theodopulos nodded.

'I'll be sure to give some consideration to what you've said,' Kosta said.

And that's likely! Ellie thought grimly. How could she expect a man like Alexander Kosta to understand that the very thing that made Lefkis unique was about to be diluted by him, until the culture of the island, as well as the delicate balance of life in the sea, no longer existed? 'You can't go ahead without consultation—'

'I can do what I like, since I own the island,' he pointed out. 'I have made the necessary investigations, and I have concluded that the deep-water harbour can't be wasted. The revenue from visiting yachts alone—'

'Profit. It all boils down to money with you—'

'If only I had the luxury of being an idealist—'

'But you do,' Ellie protested. 'Can't you see? You could have it all—'

'I think you'll find that my way, the calm and reasoned way, will work better,' Alexander insisted, not missing the opportunity to point out that she was losing control. 'The influx of visitors means every one of those deep-water berths will be required. You should be pleased, Ellie. The shallow harbour I have reserved for you and for the other fishing boats will be ideal for your purpose.'

'Say you!'

'I have decided this,' Alexander confirmed steadily, holding Ellie's impassioned gaze.

'Don't you care that the fishing fleet has considered this harbour to be its home for centuries?'

'That's not strictly true…'

There was triumph, and humour too, on Alexander's face, and even Kiria Theodopulos flinched a little at that last point. Ellie wasn't totally sure of her facts; she had only lived on Lefkis for the past eight years, and now, maddeningly, her eyes had filled with tears. The truth was she loved her simple life on the island and she couldn't bear to see anything change. It hadn't taken much for a few hotheads amongst the locals to provoke her into action. 'You can't sweep generations of tradition away and expect Lefkis to retain its charm,' she pointed out more calmly, thankful for an agreeing tilt of Kiria Theodopulos's head.

'When I require your advice, Ellie, I'll be sure to ask for it—'

'Why bother when you'd only ignore it?'

'Anticipating my actions again, Ellie?'

'Someone should stand up to you—'

'And that person's you?'

'Why not me?' Ellie said, firming her jaw as Alexander rose out of his chair.

'Ellie Mendoras? A one-woman army?'

'If I must be.' It was a pity her voice quavered at that point, and an even bigger pity she had to crane her neck in order to hold his gaze.

He moved so fast she gasped out loud as he came towards her.

'Tea?' he said, reaching past her to ring a bell.

He asked Kiria Theodopulos the same question and, having received a positive response, flashed Ellie a triumphant glance. Oh, yes, everything appeared to be going Alexander Kosta's way.

Was she strong enough to stand up to him? Ellie wondered as Alexander took up position in front of one of the picture windows. Only time would tell. So far he seemed totally unconcerned by everything that had happened.

He might have been fresh from the shower. Effortlessly elegant and perfectly groomed, he had made her feel doubly drab. A fact that shouldn't concern her at all, but for some reason did.

'May I make one small suggestion?' he said, indicating that he would whatever she thought.

As they all sat down at the tea table Ellie could only incline her head in agreement and force a smile. But her eyes told Alexander a rather different story.

'Don't make threats to me you can't honour, Ellie.'

He spoke so pleasantly even Kiria Theodopulos smiled.

It was a relief when the steward put the tray of tea in front of them and stopped her relatiating. The man's whispering presence gave Ellie the chance to look around. She had expected everything on board Alexander's yacht was of the best, and it was, but everything was restrained to the point of being boring. It was as if in spite of his massive wealth Alexander had no real interest in material objects.

You would look in vain for some sign of frivolity or excess here, Ellie concluded. Everything, including the master of the *Olympus,* took itself very seriously indeed. The pictures might have been gathered by an expert in classical art, and the colour scheme was muted. There was no relief, from the thick taupe carpet underfoot, to the few ornaments scattered about. They were all in shades of bronze, ivory or pewter-grey. The emphasis on leather and polished wood also added to the sombre atmosphere.

Nothing twinkled.

But that was her style too! In some strange way, Ellie realised, the interior of Alexander's fabulous yacht mirrored her austere lifestyle on board the simple fishing boat. This was more opulent, obviously, but the environment in which Alexander both lived and worked was contained and controlled to within an inch of its life, just like her own spartan accommodation. It was as if neither of them wanted to draw attention, though for vastly different reasons, of course…

It was quite a shock to recognise these similarities between them. She didn't enjoy the comparison. Wiping her hands self-consciously on her working clothes, Ellie was forced to admit they were hardly frivolous. The truth was she didn't possess a single item of clothing, or anything else for that matter, that wasn't functional.

'Can I get you anything else?' Alexander glanced at his wrist-watch as she drained her cup.

The meeting was over, so she had to press for a result. 'I'm just looking for an assurance that you will take the views of the islanders into consideration before you make any changes that might affect them.'

'What makes you think that I won't do that?'

When she didn't flash back an answer he relaxed. He was over his initial irritation and could see her uses. In fact, Ellie Mendoras had come along at the perfect time. She was the ideal person to win over any remaining dissenters on the island. 'You have five minutes to tell me where your main concerns lie,' he said.

Patience didn't come easily to him, but in this instance it would be worth it. Plus, she was easy on the eye and he was determined to find out everything he could about her. His usual sources had drawn a blank. The locals either knew nothing, or would tell him nothing; the time had come to make his own enquiries.

Everyone had their price, even Ellie Mendoras, Alexander reflected as she talked. She would sail her ramshackle boat to the harbour he had chosen for her, and she would keep her nose out of his business; he was determined on that. So how had this feisty local girl got under his skin? He flashed a glance at Kiria Theodopulos, who had returned to her comfortable seat overlooking the ocean. She was a safeguard, without being an intrusion. Her presence was as much a precaution for him as it was for Ellie. He'd seen too many men in his position trapped by young women who engineered a meeting only to sell their fabricated kiss-and-tell stories some time later. He'd suffered the only deception he intended to at the hands of a woman, and had no intention of repeating that mistake.

Alexander's gaze returned to Ellie, who was still talking earnestly. He was barely listening to her. Instead he was inwardly celebrating that he had pulled the rug from her feet with such remarkable ease. How had she thought she could confront him, and even shame him in front of a crowd of people, all of whom owed their livelihoods to him? Such naïvety was rare. He put it down to the fact that she had hidden herself away from the world since her father had drowned. Why else had his enquiries about her been met with a wall of silence?

He shifted position restlessly. Naïve or not, she had forgotten the first rule of commerce, which was that he who paid the piper called the tune. He wasn't going to change his mind about the power-boat races or anything else, including his decision to relocate the fishing fleet… He had been enjoying watching her face growing increasingly animated as she talked, but it was time to wrap this up; she'd had her five minutes. 'When did you say you intended leaving your mooring?'

'I didn't…' She paled. 'You haven't been listening to a word I've said, have you, Alexander?'

He got up and walked to the window. He'd been sitting down long enough. Ellie Mendoras was out of her depth trying to stand against him. Someone should have warned her that it wasn't his way to swat mosquitoes when he could afford to drain a swamp and have a road built through it.

'I think you care more about the celebrities you can attract to Lefkis than the people who actually live here,' she accused him.

He'd heard enough and rounded on her, eyes blazing. 'You're not qualified to make judgements like that. What do you know about how I feel? I beg your pardon, Kiria Theodopulos,' he was forced to add as his words split the silence. Fortunately, the old lady kept her face carefully averted.

'I feel sorry for you, Alexander—'

'Oh, do you?' He glared back at Ellie. Didn't she ever give up? 'Well, you can spare me your pity.'

He spun on his heel, turning his back on her, and then stood motionless, staring out of the window. Her continued defiance made his spine tingle. He was acutely aware of her as a woman. He wanted to take this passion somewhere else. Fast. Have her up against a wall to ease his tension. 'This meeting's over,' he said coldly. Lucky for him that reason took over.

He was on the point of delivering an ultimatum when his glance clashed with the raisin-black stare of Kiria Theodopulos. OK, for her sake and for her sake alone he would offer one more olive branch. 'Didn't my agent explain that together with a peppercorn rent for your new mooring you will be well compensated?'

Whatever he had been expecting in response, it wasn't this. Balling her hands into fists, Ellie came towards him.

'One stroke of your pen—that's all it takes for you to change someone's life, isn't it? Well, let me tell you something, Alexander; you won't get away with this—'

'It's a perfectly reasonable offer.' He looked at Kiria Theodopulos for support, only to find that the old lady seemed to have gone conveniently deaf. 'You're taking up a berth—'

'That could be better used by one of your gas-guzzling, planet-wrecking monstrosities?' Throwing her head back in disgust, Ellie uttered a heartfelt sound of contempt.

As the sunlight caught her auburn hair it blazed like fire. He could picture it spread out on a pillow in all its gleaming abundance... He quickly blanked the thought. 'I have to think about the economy of this island and the prosperity that an annual influx of wealthy visitors and their boats can bring—'

'Boats?' She cut him off. 'These things aren't boats.' She gestured around in a manner worthy of any Greek. 'They take no skill to sail with their computerised systems, their radar and autopilot! You're a Greek, Alexander! How could you support these...?'

'Monstrosities?' he supplied evenly. 'Yachts this size are increasingly a fact of life, and there's nothing you can do about it.'

She bit down on her lip. Her eyes filled with tears. For the first time in his life he wanted to back off rather than press on to victory.

He quickly got over it. Allowing her a moment to compose herself, he offered her a fresh, neatly pressed handkerchief. 'Pull yourself together,' he said brusquely.

Sniffing loudly and indelicately, she refused it. Tilting her head with pride, she informed him, 'My father used that berth all his life. The people who live around the harbour knew and loved him, and now they know me...'

And would love her, he realised with a blow to his solar plexus. 'Time moves on, Ellie, and we must move with it...'

'Time?' Her brow was wrinkled as she considered this. 'So the heritage of this island means nothing to you? You bought Lefkis and now it's yours to do with as you like?'

'That's right,' he said, relieved that she was starting to see sense.

'Then I dread the consequences,' she told him gravely.

'I think you'd better explain yourself,' he threatened.

'If Lefkis is the latest toy in your toy box, what happens when you tire of the island, Alexander? Will you just toss it out of the playpen?'

'I'm not going to dignify that comment with a reply.'

Her response was to jut out her chin in a way that, had she been a man, would have invited him to take a swing at it. But the issues at stake were too serious to allow this meeting to deteriorate into a game of tit for tat.

'This would never have happened in my father's time,' she said, shaking her head as if he was in the wrong.

It was time for a few home truths. 'In your father's time there was no clinic on the island. There was no hospital, no secondary school and people died from influenza before a doctor could arrive by sea from another island. In your father's time Lefkis was a poverty-stricken pile of rocks where people scratched a living the best way they could—'

'But they stayed,' she argued passionately. 'And why do you think that was, Alexander?'

Before he could tell her they had nowhere else to go, she gave him her version of events.

'They stayed on because Lefkis was their home, their community, their family. They stayed on because they love the island as I do. Are the fiestas a recent custom? No. They've been held on Lefkis for hundreds of years. Do the tourists crowd in to witness some stage show contrived to strip them of their money before they leave? Are these people actors, or shallow charlatans?' As she pointed to Kiria Theodopulos, her mouth worked with emotion. 'Is that what you believe, Alexander?' Her eyes blazed into his. 'Because if you do, you'll never be worthy to call yourself a son of Lefkis, even if you do own the island—'

'Have you finished?' he said coldly. 'Good; then let me explain something. My success is founded on the solid rock of self-belief. That and sound judgement. This island is going to change. I *will* bring power-boat racing. I *will* clear the deep-water harbour in order to accommodate the bigger vessels. And I will *not* risk the future prosperity of Lefkis in order to humour you and a few local hotheads!' Or to placate Kiria Theodopulos, whom he noticed now had reached up to clasp Ellie's hand.

The silence in the room climbed to a new level as they stared at each other. He had let loose more emotion in these last few minutes than he had in years. And emotion had always been his enemy.

CHAPTER THREE

HE RANG a bell discreetly with his foot. It brought the steward hurrying back. 'You may take the tea tray away now,' he told him. 'We're finished here.'

'I'm not finished,' Ellie asserted, glancing at the steward's retreating back.

'I am,' he told her coldly. Striding past her, he opened the door. 'Accept what you have been told, or you'll hear from my agent again. I'd like to keep this friendly, but…'

She got the message. He didn't need to say anything more. Realisation dawned swiftly behind her eyes. This wasn't just a question of a berth for her fishing boat, or a power-boat race or anything else that might concern her—it had come down to a decision as to whether or not she would be allowed to remain living on the island.

Instead of crumbling into misery she stared at him with an expression of undiluted fury in her eyes. Then, stalking stiff-legged across the room, she came to join him at the door.

He stood back to allow her to pass. As he did so he caught a whiff of her scent: soap, sea and engine oil. It was something he would never forget. Surprisingly, he found it quite a winning combination. Wisely he kept his wandering thoughts to himself and confined himself to a curt nod of dismissal.

'Goodbye, Kirie Kosta,' Ellie intoned with matching formality.

She met his gaze fearlessly. Her mouth was compressed in an angry line and her eyes were still blazing fire at him. She stood in front of him long enough for him to notice that her curly hair was sun-streaked to the point of being blonde at the temples, and however hard she tried to flatten those lips they still curved in a perfect Cupid's bow.

'Kiria Theodopulos?' she said, looking past him into the room.

He had forgotten the old lady was even there, and yet he noticed everything about Ellie. There was a smudge of oil on her cheek that drew his attention back to the ugly scar… As she brought her hand up to cover it he wondered at the shame she was feeling—the shame that showed in her eyes. It puzzled him. It even softened him, just a little. 'Make an appointment if you want to see me again,' he said gruffly as the two women walked past him.

'When can I see you?' Ellie demanded like a shot.

'My PA keeps my diary.' He refused to be pressured by a child. She looked so young standing beside Kiria Theodopulos…and, of course, good Greek manners dictated that he should escort the old lady back to the shore. This wasn't over yet. He offered his arm to Kiria Theodopulos, and when she took it Ellie had no option but to follow on behind.

When they reached the shore something made him throw Ellie a lifeline. 'I'm holding a meeting tomorrow. You should attend. It's on neutral territory,' he added with some irony.

'Where?' She looked at him with interest.

'In the council building.'

'I know it.'

Her remorseless enthusiasm for her cause niggled at him. 'It's at eleven. Miss it and you won't get a second chance.'

'Thank you,' she said, as if he had offered her something graciously.

Maybe he should have added that she would get a hearing by people on his payroll, but why not let her find that out for herself? It might have more impact that way; show her she was defending a lost cause. 'Do you have a problem?' he said, realising she was still standing there, looking thoughtful.

'My wardrobe is somewhat limited.'

The elders of Lefkis were a formal group who wouldn't take kindly to someone turning up in a boiler suit—even if that someone was Ellie. 'I have a secretary who might be prepared to lend you something to wear,' he offered.

'I can afford my own clothes, thank you, Kirie Kosta,' she said, tilting that chin of hers again.

'Alexander,' he reminded her. 'And don't be late.'

'I'll be there,' she assured him with suppressed excitement.

This was just the opportunity she had been waiting for—what a shame, he thought; it really wouldn't do her any good. 'Ellie…'

'Yes?'

He had been about to offer her an advance on the compensation she would receive for quitting her berth to give her funds to buy some formal clothes, but why should he? Why not let her climb out of the hole she'd dug herself? 'Forget it,' he said.

'You will let me speak tomorrow?' she said suspiciously.

'You'll never know if you don't turn up, will you?'

Her eyes were round and wounded. He moved in for the kill. 'If you'd troubled to read the papers my agent served on you, you would know the compensation I'm paying is enough for you to buy a whole new wardrobe of clothes *and* the best boat on the market—'

'I already own the best boat on the market. And as for money, contrary to what you believe, it counts for nothing here—'

'Oh, really? So the economy of this island works on a different system from the rest of the world? Get real, Ellie. Come to the meeting, or call it a day. It's the only offer on the table—'

'And if I don't like the outcome?'

He gave her a look.

'I have no right of appeal, is that right?'

She understood now.

No right of appeal? Ellie fumed. So, Lefkis was about to become a dictatorship under the heel of Alexander Kosta. Having survived the rule of one tyrant, it was going to suffer another. Her mind was in ferment as she walked briskly down the quay. Maybe she had been too long on an island surrounded by people she could trust and had lost her sense of what was and what wasn't acceptable behaviour, but Alexander Kosta had really gone too far.

And she was going to take him on single-handedly?

Yes, if she had to; what other option did she have?

Ellie glanced up as she reached her berth. She had been distracted by the braying laughter coming from the towering white yacht moored up next to her boat. The occupants of the super-yacht would be well into their champagne by now, which meant she had another sleepless night to look forward to.

And how would Alexander sleep? Ellie wondered, gazing back at the *Olympus*. The last thing she wanted to think about was Alexander stretched out on his palatial bed, but...

Perhaps he never slept. Perhaps he just stood by the window, staring out at his well-packed marina, gloating over the revenue the super-yachts would bring him.

Taking hold of the familiar rope that said she was home,

Ellie ground her teeth in anger as she padded lightly up the gangway. She was wasting her time imagining Alexander might one day change and use all that power he wielded for good. But she'd have another go, tomorrow at the meeting. And as for wondering if that stern face of his ever cracked a smile…

Perhaps he didn't have any teeth… She laughed to herself.

Buoyed up by that thought, Ellie strode purposefully across the deck. Closing the hatch door behind her as she climbed down the companionway, she bolted it securely. Alexander wasn't the only one in Lefkis who kept his life locked up tight.

Turning on the low-voltage lights that made everything so cosy, Ellie started making plans for the meeting. She suspected Alexander was only humouring her, with his decision about the race and the harbour already made, but still, she had to try to shake people out of their apathy. If she didn't succeed Alexander's stranglehold on the island would be complete.

Reaching inside her neatly stowed fridge, she got out a carton of milk and poured a glass. Moving back across the cabin to the porthole, she peered out. She could see the *Olympus*, where no doubt right now Alexander was busy ticking off another tame local willing to rubber-stamp his ideas. Big mistake. She tipped her glass in an ironic salute.

But there was nowhere else she would rather be, so she had to tread carefully and at least appear to play by his rules. The neighbouring islands were just as beautiful as Lefkis, but they didn't exert the same hold over her. Not that she wanted to become part of some ritzy set-up, which seemed to be Alexander's plan for Lefkis.

Ellie pulled back from the window. The thought of more conflict with Alexander had made her heart thunder uncontrollably. She'd seen the lights of the *Olympus* reflected in the water. Could Alexander see her staring at him?

Ridiculous! Of course he couldn't…

Rinsing out her glass, she put it away, then, going to the small tin where she kept her cash, she counted it out. There was enough 'just in case' money to buy a cheap two-piece at the market, and maybe a pair of proper shoes as well…

She was on time, which he might have expected, but what on earth was she wearing? Alexander's discerning gaze swept over Ellie's market-stall outfit. The jacket, in an alarming shade of sludge-green, was far too small for her. Under that was a hideous pink nylon lace top. He couldn't remember ever seeing anything quite so horrendous. But on the plus side he hadn't seen her breasts before, and now he could see them clearly beneath the close-fitting top. They were large *and* pert. Very nice…

He dragged his gaze away to consider a skirt so big it had swung around her hips, leaving the slit that was supposed to be at the back at the side. She looked a mess. Not that the elderly man currently showing her to her seat seemed to notice…

He had arranged for her to sit on the front row, right under his gaze and where he could keep an eye on her. Why was the usher taking so long to settle her? What did they find to talk and laugh about? She looked relaxed. Too relaxed.

One thing puzzled him. It was clear she knew the elderly usher, but he was holding on to her arm in his enthusiasm when she'd panicked at the thought of his bodyguards touching her. It was another piece of the puzzle like the scar on her cheek…

Alexander frowned as he organised the papers in front of him. He had no time to waste on Ellie Mendoras today. She'd have her chance to speak and that would be an end of it.

* * *

'Ms Mendoras, sit down. It isn't your turn to speak yet.' He couldn't believe she was causing trouble again. She should realise that everyone here was in his camp. Maybe she did, but that hadn't stopped her protesting. 'Ms Mendoras!' His voice cracked out like a blow with a gavel.

'Mr Kosta,' she rapped back at him to a murmur of general surprise. 'This audience is largely composed of visitors to the island, all of whom have a vested interest in being here. I speak for the locals—'

'I think I know that—'

'Profit is the only goal of the newcomers you have introduced to the island,' she went on, ignoring him. 'These races of yours—'

'Will take place. Now sit down, Ms Mendoras, before I have you removed from the chamber—'

'Am I the only person here who cares about this island?' she demanded, ignoring him as she gazed passionately around the packed council chamber.

She was certainly the only person present holding their shoes in their hand. 'I'm warning you,' he tried for one last time, 'sit down now, or I'll have you ejected.'

Her look suggested, you and whose army? And as he held her fiery gaze he wanted to be the one to cart her out, but he wouldn't deposit her on the pavement—he would keep walking until they reached his bed. 'I'll tell you when it's your turn to speak.'

'You will?' she panted tensely.

'Yes, I will,' he confirmed briskly. 'Now, can we get on?'

Reluctantly, she sat down.

Ellie twisted the fabric of her skirt as she waited for her turn. So far she hadn't heard anything to reassure her. What was worse, Alexander wouldn't stop staring at her. Shouldn't he be paying attention to whomever was talking at the time?

Ellie dipped her head to avoid Alexander's gaze, but when she looked up again he was still staring at her. She firmed her jaw. She had every right to be here, and to be heard. And hadn't she, in fact, come at his personal invitation? Who was going to stand up against him if she didn't? She had to save Lefkis from Alexander.

And save Alexander from himself?

A rush of awareness pulsed through her at the thought. She was prepared to hold her hands up right now on that one; Alexander would have to save himself.

No one had listened to a word she'd said. Her audience had grown restless and impatient. No one wanted to hear about conservation issues or anything else that might skim the cream off their profit. He almost felt sorry for her as she stood up to go. She knew she had failed. She knew he had seen her fail. She had played her hand and had received muted applause for her trouble. Even if anyone had agreed with her everyone was frightened of offending him.

He caught up with her outside. 'Hey…'

'What do you want?' She turned defensively, still prepared to do battle.

He looked at the angle of her chin and the rigidity of her shoulders. She was hurt. Hurt that no one had listened to her, not even the elders she cared so much about. Everything had worked out in his favour. He could have told her that was what would happen and saved her the trouble of coming. 'I just wanted to make sure that this little protest of yours is over—'

'Over?' she cut across him acidly.

'Don't be silly, Ellie!' he exclaimed with frustration, seeing the fight in her eyes. 'Progress is essential, even on a small island like Lefkis. Without it everything comes to a standstill. You don't want that, do you?'

'I don't want you...undiluted you, deciding what the rest of us should have to accept in our daily lives. I don't want Lefkis becoming a place where people who aren't rich or famous aren't welcome. I don't want the island I know and love becoming a satellite of your ivory tower—a multi-million-pound playground for you to dip into whenever you're feeling bored.' She marched on, refusing to turn and look at him.

'And if we follow your plan,' he said, keeping in step with her, 'a slow-down in the economy here will be followed by steady decline. The young people, the lifeblood of the island, will be forced to emigrate in search of jobs, leaving the old people to fend for themselves. Is that what you want, Ellie? Ellie! Stop walking away from me!' Gripping her shoulders, he turned her to face him. Her eyes blazed in passionate fury. 'I won't allow that to happen. I have to provide full employment...' But as he spoke he realised he was no longer interested in words. He was consumed by her—her passion, her fight, her attempt to show her disinterest in him.

Under his dark scrutiny her gaze wavered. He steered her into the shadows, away from all the curious eyes. His gaze dropped to her lips. The chemistry between them was electric; irresistible...

Kissing Ellie was like finding harbour after an endless voyage. It was more sex and lust than a week in bed with any normal woman. She resisted him to begin with; he'd expected that. But then her hands went round his neck, and she dragged him close. The kiss was hot, angry—driven by their need and frustration. Her abandon startled him; delighted him. But it was also his cue to back right off. He couldn't afford to lose control.

Turning his face away from her, he wiped his mouth with the back of his hand. He was almost desperate to eradicate the taste of her. He doubted he'd ever succeed. She'd tasted fresh and young and eager and innocent. And he wanted her.

'Is that supposed to keep me quiet?' she asked him with contempt in her voice.

He looked at her; she was shaking, but not from fear.

'This is going nowhere—'

'You think I'd want it to?' she asked incredulously, while her body told him something else.

He watched her stalk away with a heady mix of lust and relief. That was Ellie Mendoras over and done with. His attention was needed elsewhere. Business called and, in his world, business always came first.

What had she done? Ellie touched her lips again, tentatively, and then went to look at them in the mirror. She traced them cautiously with her fingertip. They were still swollen and very pink, and the delicate skin around them was still a little sore where Alexander's beard had abraded her.

And even now, so long after The Kiss, she was still trembling, her heart was still racing and she was still aroused. What frightened her even more than her inexplicable lapse of good sense was the way Alexander had quite suddenly switched off. One minute he had been kissing her in the most bone-melting way, and the next standing aloof, staring at her coldly as if nothing at all had happened. OK, so her behaviour could be comfortably classified as insane, but his emotional detachment was chilling. What had happened to him? Could money do that to you?

Ellie turned from the mirror knowing she had too much work ahead of her to dwell on how stupid she'd been. She had put herself at risk when she of all people knew better, and had allowed Alexander to think she was easy. It was time to get her life back on track.

He saw her first. He guessed she was stocking up on provisions for that day's trip. He had to question the thump in his guts when he first caught sight of her. He tipped his sunglasses down his nose, then settled them straight again before getting on with the job of policing the moorings. He was checking up on the new safety provisions he'd put in place for the crowded harbour...

Was he? Was he really? Didn't he have scores of people who could do that for him?

He brushed all thoughts of what had happened between them aside as he strolled up to her. He blocked out the way she'd felt, the way she'd tasted, the way she'd made him feel. He replaced all those thoughts with anger, mostly directed at himself. 'I thought you would have gone by now.'

'I'm sorry to disappoint you, Alexander.'

He glanced pointedly in the direction of her boat.

'My time isn't up.'

She held his gaze to repeat her assertion that he didn't frighten her. Interesting that she was trembling.

'I'd love to stay and talk, Alexander,' she lied, 'but as you can see I've got a trip to prepare for. My last trip from this harbour.'

Having got this last dig in, she moved away.

'Fully booked, I hope?'

'Yes...'

She didn't look round, but the tension was still there in her shoulders, even though he knew her chin would be tipped at a defiant angle. He guessed she'd walk up and down with a sandwich board on her back if that was what it took to drum up business from her new mooring. 'If your tours are so popular you shouldn't have any problem persuading your clientele to follow you across the island—'

'Let's hope you're right,' she called back to him.

If looks could kill he was a dead man. She was playing him at his own game, acting as if they'd never met, never touched, never kissed, and all that with a world of passion driving them. 'I thought you had more confidence than that—'

'I've got all the confidence I need, Alexander,' she assured him, tossing her hair in defiance as she walked away.

He wasn't finished yet; no one walked away from him. 'I'm having a dinner party on board the *Olympus* tonight—'

'Enjoy…'

'Why don't you come along?' Better to keep her where he knew what she was doing than allow her to spread her dissent through those he had already converted to his way.

She hesitated; then turned around. Her brow was puckered as if in thought. 'Well, that's a real shame, Alexander. I won't be able to make it tonight. You see, my tour won't return in time…'

His lips tightened. The last thing he had expected was to be turned down flat. 'This event will last well into the night,' he said, walking up to her. 'Please yourself, Ellie.' Their faces were dangerously close. He shrugged and drew back as she stared up at him. If she wanted a fight she'd picked the right person.

He watched her walk away down the quay—proud, defiant, passionate, and asking to be laid. He could wait. Life was a game of chess. The only problem for Ellie was his life was the only game he cared about.

CHAPTER FOUR

AND anyway, I've got nothing to wear, Ellie told herself as she moved about the boat, making the last of her preparations for her tour.

I'm sure you have, her inner voice argued. What's wrong with what you're wearing now?

Market-stall clothes? A cheap cotton top and shorts? Every girl knew that was the dream outfit for dinner on board a billionaire's yacht. Not that she had the slightest intention of attending Alexander's party, of course. She hadn't lost her hold on reason altogether.

Turning Alexander's invitation down flat and seeing surprise flash across those hard green eyes had been worth every moment of her one-off loss of control when he'd kissed her. And a one-off it had to be. Not that she hadn't replayed The Kiss over and over in her mind, but in those daydreams it had been safe to kiss him, because Alexander had been magically transformed into a pleasant, reasonable man and she, of course, had become Miss Sensible, who knew just where to draw the line.

And now it was time to draw the line under her daydreams altogether, Ellie told herself firmly. With the keenest of her group expected on board any minute she still had some final checks to complete.

Everything looked good. The radio was playing up and there was no time to fix it, but as she wouldn't be going out of signal range her mobile phone would do. She kept it primed with all the emergency numbers she could possibly need. She had cleaned every inch of the boat, and the ingredients for lunch—pasta with a fresh tomato sauce and cheese along with home-baked bread and crisp green salad—were stowed away in the refrigerator in the galley. Planting her hands on her hips, Ellie surveyed her kingdom. It looked as if she was ready.

The success of her tours had exceeded Ellie's wildest expectations. It was a wrench to think this would be her last trip from the main harbour, but at least she was going out with a bang—no thanks to Alexander. Ten people had booked, which was the maximum number she could take on board.

Glancing at the notice to quit she had received from his agent soon wiped the smile off her face. Forty-eight hours to arrange everything and say goodbye to the harbour where her father's boat had been berthed for generations was nothing short of an insult.

Alexander hadn't wasted a second when he bought the island, Ellie reflected angrily, gripping the rough hessian ropes at the sides of the companionway as she headed back on deck. Fortunately it would take him a little longer than that to turn Lefkis into the billionaire's playground he envisaged, by which time the locals would have surely have rallied and found the courage they needed to keep him on a leash.

Ellie's mouth was set in a flat line of fury. She had discovered chains across the channel barring the free passage of her boat. What an outrage! It was unbelievable!

Turning, she made her apologies to her passengers. She explained that this was where they were supposed to have been dropping anchor and having lunch. It was a struggle not to show what she felt about it. This was a favourite spot, a sheltered bay where even children and the weakest swimmers in her group could snorkel in safety. But a newly painted sign stabbed into the side of the cliff announced in both Greek and English that entry to the bay without a permit was forbidden. No need to wonder by whose authority that order had been issued!

There was no point in dwelling on it, she'd just have to move on and find another bay. She owed her passengers a happy day, and Alexander wasn't going to spoil that for them.

The open sea soothed her and everyone wanted to ask her about the tiny creatures she would collect as soon as they stopped. It was a nice group of people, and she soon forgot what had happened—until a speedboat cut right across her path.

'What now?' Ellie murmured angrily, noticing the Kosta insignia on the side of the boat.

And now his bodyguards were actually waving her away. Did they think he had acquired the ocean along with the island? Incredible!

Ellie swung the wheel to avoid a collision, but the small, fast boat continued to plague her, crisscrossing in front and behind, and causing such turbulence with its wake she began to fear for the safety of her passengers.

This was intolerable, Ellie fumed. Not only had she been forced to sail to the other side of the island, but now her passengers had been put at risk too. Plus, by the time they dropped anchor there would hardly be any time to swim before she had to start back again.

She would have to offer a full refund, not that the money concerned her. It was Alexander's high-handed behaviour that really made her mad. Perhaps she would go to his high-tone party and tell him exactly what she thought of him in front of his guests…

Ellie had mellowed a little by the time the harbour lights came into view. She always felt the same deep sense of contentment when she returned to her mooring. It was the feeling of a job well done, and a day well spent. She guessed this was the feeling every sailor knew when they saw their home port looming. Little was she to know that another shock awaited her.

Instead of an empty berth there was a huge super-yacht taking up her space!

Calmly reassuring everyone, she altered course. As the harbour was full, the only place she could safely disembark her passengers was at the ferry port. It meant a longer walk for them, and a substantial temporary-docking fee. She would send back in a taxi all those who wanted one, Ellie determined, and make sure her expenses were reimbursed. She gave a long, hard stare at the *Olympus*.

Alexander must have known what would happen when she had met him down on the harbour front. Why hadn't he said anything? This was wholly accountable. Her time on the eviction notice hadn't expired yet.

As Ellie helped one of her family groups into the waiting taxi she threw a murderous look in the direction of the *Olympus*. The family was burdened down with knapsacks and towels and cut a stark contrast to the wealthy visitors on the super-yachts with their entourages of staff. No doubt Alexander wouldn't approve of tourists who had to carry their own things around. It seemed you had to have a certain bank balance and a certain way of life to be welcome on Lefkis these days.

Having seen the family safely into the taxi and paid their fare in advance, Ellie made sure the few remaining passengers were happy to walk back into town before considering what to do next. It was almost dark, which meant it was too late to sail to the other side of the island and find her new berth. Her best option was to drop anchor in the harbour and hope that if any of the mammoth yachts decided to move in the night their captains would notice her.

Weighing anchor, she cast off and cruised slowly into the middle of the harbour. Music from a live combo on board the *Olympus* drifted over to her. It seemed to mock her. She should have accepted that invitation and then she could have confronted Alexander right away. No doubt he was having a whale of a time. Nothing unpleasant must be allowed to tarnish the master of Lefkis's pleasure.

A soft breeze ruffled Ellie's hair as she stood by the mast. It would be so easy to pack up, sail away and admit defeat. She stared up at the *Olympus*. And allow Alexander to get away with what he'd done? Not a chance!

Having lowered her inflatable into the water, Ellie chugged steadfastly back to shore. Unfortunately, her lack of an invitation to Alexander's party meant it wouldn't be easy to get on board. She was hardly dressed for the occasion, and wasn't surprised when the security guards turned her away.

For a couple of wild moments she contemplated slipping past them by mingling with the other guests. There was a steady procession of glamorous, expensively dressed people moving past her. They were allowed up the gangway with barely a glance at the invitations they were holding out for inspection. Stewards were waiting to greet them at the top with flutes of champagne, carried on silver trays... Why shouldn't she give it a go?

But when she tried to pass herself off as one of the glitterati she was immediately shunned. She could see the guests exchanging glances, as if poverty were a disease that might be catching.

She had to admit she didn't look her best, and hadn't thought this through properly. She didn't even have any make-up on, and her face was reddened by the wind. A good douse of perfume would come in handy too—to mask the faint but unmistakable tang of engine oil.

Retreating into the shadows, Ellie considered what to do next. Right now, running back to her cosy cabin and burying her head beneath a pillow seemed the most attractive option, but her stubborn self would never allow her to do that.

She would just have to find another way to get on board, Ellie thought as she gazed up at the super-yacht. The *Olympus* was lit from stem to stern with fairy lights, and was a magnificent sight; awe-inspiring. But she wasn't beaten yet...

First there were man-mountain security guards to get past, and then hundreds of fabulously dressed people on board. She'd stand out like a sore thumb. The task she'd set herself was impossible...

As some local girls trouped past Ellie perked up. They were all dressed as waitresses in neat black dresses and crisply starched white pinafores and caps. They had obviously been hired for the evening to serve at a dinner following the champagne reception...

Leaping from her hiding place, she waved to them and called out. When they saw her they stopped. Ellie put her suggestion to the girl closest in size to herself. The young girl laughed at first, and asked if she was serious. When Ellie confirmed that she was the girl consulted with her friends and finally agreed.

Yes, she was perfectly serious, Ellie thought, gazing at her reflection in the mirror of the ladies' room at the café. She had given the girl the night off, plus the dainty gold chain she always wore round her neck as a thank-you. It had been her mother's, and was hard to part with, but curbing Alexander's megalomania before he ruined the island had to be her primary concern.

Getting on board now was easy. She was allowed to walk up the narrow gangway at the stern of the yacht with all the other temporary staff. Fooling the *maître d'*, Luigi, was rather more difficult, and there was a worrying interlude when he questioned her about her previous work experience. Fortunately, time was pressing down on Luigi just as it was for Ellie, and finally he let her go.

There was such a crush on board it was possible to escape even Luigi's eagle eye, and after a short but busy time helping to serve drinks Ellie found herself swept along with everyone else towards the grand salon, where the dinner that evening was being held. A honeyed radiance spilled out of the double doors. It made Ellie gasp as she entered with the guests. The retractable roof above the grand salon had been opened to the stars, and in addition to the moonlight the glitter of silver and cut glass was reflected in the soft glow of candlelight.

It was such a beautiful sight that for a moment Ellie forgot her mission. Then she tensed. There wasn't a top table to make things easy for her. The seating arrangement was intimate, with round tables set for eight. Glamorous women in sequinned designer gowns and low-cut sheaths were already being shown to their places by their elegant male companions… But where was Alexander?

'Have you nothing better to do than stand and stare?'

Ellie nearly jumped out of her skin. She had been discovered standing idle by the *maître d'*.

'Thank you, Luigi; I'll handle this…'

'Alexander!' Ellie clutched her chest. Of course it was Alexander. And did she have to sound quite so breathless and pathetic? Had she come here to swoon? No! Ellie's gaze roved over Alexander's impeccably tailored dinner jacket. Like all his clothes it skimmed his muscular frame, showing it off to best advantage, and then she noticed that his hand-tied bow-tie was undone...

'Once again you have gone to far too much trouble to engineer a meeting between us,' he observed. 'Why is that, Ellie?'

Ellie had to force her gaze from buttons she longed to fasten to hide Alexander's tanned skin, and from a tie she longed to secure rather too tightly around his neck. 'I'm sorry, did you say something?'

'You could make a start by not staring at me. You're drawing attention to yourself.'

'Oh, really?' And did she care? But Alexander did. Seeing their billionaire host chatting to a waitress was causing quite a bit of interest.

'I thought I offered you a formal invitation for this evening.'

'You know you did. You also know that I refused.'

'So you changed your mind...'

Did he have to speak to her in that husky, intimate way, with his lips tugging up at one corner in a way that made her feel all at odds inside?

Perhaps she was wrong about Alexander, Ellie realised, taking a step back to a safer distance. Perhaps it was she who cared that people were staring at them. He merely seemed amused.

'Did I mention fancy dress?' he said, maintaining a straight face.

'I'm not here to enjoy myself, Alexander. This was the only way I could get on board—'

'You must have been keen.'

'I think we should go somewhere else to talk. Somewhere quieter,' she added pointedly.

'Can't whatever this is wait? I have a party to host—'

'No, it cannot wait,' she rapped back at him.

'So, where do you suggest? My private suite?'

In spite of her outward bravado, Ellie quailed. There was no Kiria Theodopulos to protect her this time.

She remained beside the door.

'Come in, I won't bite.'

Or if I do, you'll enjoy it, Alexander's mocking eyes seemed to promise Ellie.

Even as her bones turned to liquid heat she glanced at the door handle, working out how quickly she could turn it and escape if she had to.

She sucked in some deep, steadying breaths, trying to ignore the way Alexander always made her feel. She tried listening to the muted classical guitar music playing softly in the background. She even tried willing her heart to beat in time. But still it raced. And her nipples had become achingly hard beneath her uniform. Sensation was pooling at the apex of her thighs, and in every way she was aroused.

This was insane. She couldn't have sex with any man, let alone with Alexander. Bracketing him and sex together in her mind was madness.

As she struggled to calm down she turned her attention to the salon and everything it contained. The room was discreetly lit with cream leather sofas facing each other across a jewel-coloured Persian rug. The scent of fresh flowers pervaded everything. There was a low floral arrangement on a table dividing the sofas, and a more exuberant display in a dramatic blue and white vase balanced on a tall plinth in one corner of the room...

But she wasn't here to write an article for *Beautiful Homes*!

'Do you have any idea what's happening in *your* harbour,

Alexander? Or have *you* been too busy enjoying yourself to notice?' It came out like acid when she had planned to be incisive, rational, businesslike…

'If you mean your berth?' He held her gaze. 'That was unavoidable. The ambassador arrived without warning. A great honour, as I'm sure you'll be the first to agree…'

'The ambassador…' Ellie frowned. Each time she had a justifiable complaint against him it seemed that Alexander was able to come up with a cast-iron explanation. 'But even the ambassador must know a sailor's berth is sacrosanct. It's the one thing you can be sure of when you're out at sea—'

'The ambassador takes precedence over everyone, including you, Ellie…' He liked her in a waitress's uniform. The severe cut and strait-laced style of it was very sexy. All of a sudden he wasn't interested in talk of berths and boats. He wanted a firm surface and a few hours of earthy pleasure.

'What I'm talking about is a simple matter of maritime courtesy,' she said, jerking him back to full attention.

'Simple?' He gave her a dry look. 'Life is never simple, Ellie, as you should know.'

'Not on Lefkis,' she agreed robustly. 'At least, not since you bought the island.'

This wasn't what he wanted to hear and his expression darkened. Every other woman on his yacht would have donated her clothes to charity for an opportunity like this. 'If you're only here to berate me about something I cannot change…' He made a move towards the door, and was incredulous when she stepped in front of him to stop him.

'Will not change, don't you mean?'

'Will not!' he conceded grimly, more as an order to himself.

Exhaling with frustration, she turned away. 'I might have known you wouldn't be interested in anything I have to say.'

'Then why did you come here?'

Her hesitation told him everything she didn't want to.

'Because someone has to stand up to you,' she said without turning round.

'And that someone's you?' he pressed ruthlessly. 'Who gives you permission to speak for everyone on the island, Ellie?'

'The elders.' She turned around. Her cheeks were red. 'The elders asked me.'

He started to enjoy the sparks that flew between them. Relishing the sparring, he pressed on. 'Don't you think they might have changed their minds in the interim?'

'They haven't…they wouldn't—'

'And you're quite sure about that?'

Her eyes blazed. 'No one dares say a word against you—'

'Except for you?' He raised a brow.

'That's right.' As she held his hard, taunting gaze he could see the pulse fluttering in her neck. The chemistry between them sizzled. The tension was palpable. Her cheeks were pink, her lips were plump. She looked ravishing in her neat maid's outfit; even the way she had tied her hair back to comply with the *maître d'*'s instructions suited her.

'The least your people could have given me was some notice that I was about to lose my berth—'

He didn't want her to keep talking, he wanted to drag her into his arms. He could tell she was as aroused as he was, and if he held her to him for a moment he wouldn't kiss her right away. He wanted to stare into her eyes and see them darken; he would savour every moment of her compliance. He wanted to feel her soft flesh yielding against him and hear her breathing quicken. He wanted to breathe in her scent and anticipate how she would taste. He wanted it all.

But on his terms, not hers. 'Didn't they call you on your

radio?' he said, affecting concern. 'I trust you have a working radio on board, Ellie, because if you don't that's a severe breach of the maritime protocol you're at such pains to uphold...'

His presence was overwhelming her, he could tell. He turned away, pretending not to notice the way she was propping herself up against the door with her arms outstretched, her slender fingers pressing hard into the woodwork. He bit down on his thumb to curb his smile. The chase was the best part for him; always the best part.

'My radio wasn't working,' she managed at last, 'but I carry a mobile phone—'

'And if that had been lost overboard, what then?' he said, wheeling round on her. 'Do you generally put your passengers' lives at risk?'

'Never! It was a one-off. If anyone put their lives at risk it was you—'

'Me?'

'Your drivers—your goons, your guards, whatever you like to call them...'

She flared a look at him, which he countered with a regretful smile. 'That was unfortunate,' he admitted.

'Unfortunate?'

What was happening to her? She had planned to take this calmly, and already she was in a fury. Plus, she was never slapdash at sea; never relaxed her guard on the water, or in her private life. She'd had two terrible lessons and wasn't likely to forget either of them. She operated her small business under the strictest safety conditions, but would Alexander believe that now? His calculating gaze warned her she was at risk of losing more than her berth, and, as he signed off all the work permits and licences now, he was probably right!

'This must never happen again, Ellie.'

'It won't—'

'Well, now you're here, you might as well get everything off your chest… And I don't have all day.'

As Alexander issued the reminder he rasped his hand against his chin, drawing her attention to the rough black stubble. It was a sharp contrast to the stubble of the old man who had attacked her; his had been white and had felt like an old toothbrush, but even so he'd been too strong for her—

'Are you listening to me, Ellie? I don't have time for your daydreams now.'

Daydreams? That made her memories sound so enjoyable, when they were anything but—

'You were present at the meeting. You heard me inviting comment from the floor. You saw me enter into discussion. What more do you want from me, Ellie?'

'I heard people rubber-stamp your proposals. I saw people in your pay agreeing with you. As far as I can tell that meeting was nothing more than a back-slapping exercise to make you feel good—'

'I laid out my plans in front of the elders of Lefkis, who agreed them—'

'Not all of them were there. If they had been, do you think they would have agreed to you stretching chains across channels and marking artificial boundaries in the ocean?' Ellie made a sound of contempt. 'I don't think so, Alexander.'

'Those chains were a necessary precaution to mark out the route—'

'For what?' she interrupted. 'A race that won't take place if the locals stand against you?'

'Do you think they'll find the courage to do that?'

'They will! I know they will…'

She would, he thought. 'The trials *will* take place,' he

assured her. Whether you like it or not, was something he didn't have to say. Short of a miracle Ellie knew how little influence she could bring to bear on his decision. 'Some of the channels aren't deep enough, or wide enough to allow power boats through and guides must be set. Safety is paramount—at least to me,' he added pointedly.

'You talk of safety, when all I can think about is the danger that follows in your wake. You frighten me, Alexander. I'm frightened of what you're doing to the island…'

'Frightened of change, do you mean?'

'You make changes without consideration of the consequences. You only care about yourself—'

'This isn't about me, or you; this is about the future of an island and its people.'

'Do you think I don't know that?'

The passion driving her was as great as his own, but it was time for some blunt talking. 'When I bought Lefkis the island was bankrupt, and there were no plans to rescue the situation. Did it escape your notice that Demetrios Lindos kept all the money for himself? I'm not like him, Ellie. I'm not like that man—'

'Maybe not, but as far as I'm concerned you're just another breed of megalomaniac who refuses to see anyone else's point of view. Oh, I know you think you know best for all of us, but that's your business brain talking, Alexander, not your heart.'

He stared at her. Her theory nagged at him, not that he was prepared to admit that she was right. 'I have a party to get back to,' he said impatiently, 'so if that's all…'

'No, it isn't all. You can't just dismiss me like that.'

He was just about to assure her how wrong she was when he saw her hand creep up to trace the ugly scar. He had to ask himself who would do that to a woman. Someone had; that was no accident. Ellie had roused someone to such a fury they had attacked her like a wild beast. What else had they done to her? 'I'm not dismissing you,' he said harshly as the anger migrated to his voice. 'Sit down!'

'Don't talk to me like that!'

'All right, then! Please sit down.'

He needed space from her and went to stand beside the flowers, inhaling their scent so he wouldn't have to inhale Ellie's far more preferable perfume. He had to smile to think he was beginning to find the scent of engine oil and soap addictive.

He turned around to see her still hovering, no doubt torn between calling it a day and one last stand. He had to admire her guts. 'No one will disturb us here. We're quite alone.' He might be many things, but he was not a bully. 'If you sit on the sofa you will find a call button on the table in front of you. If you feel uncomfortable at any time you can ring it, and someone will come immediately…'

Her eyes turned round and solemn as she stared at him. He sensed her fear. He had to wonder who could possibly have frightened her to this extent. It roused feelings he'd never experienced before—like the fierce need to protect. Fortunately, common sense held him back from making any rash statements to that effect.

He finally listened to what she had to say, and was shocked by what she told him about the events of the day. Intimidation had never been part of his plan. There was no honour in scoring points over a vulnerable girl, and his men should have known better than to endanger her boat. They'd told him something about what had happened, but clearly not the whole story. Putting Ellie and her passengers at risk was unforgivable, and they would be punished. He told her so. This was exactly why he felt the need to control everything. His power base had grown so vast it was open to misrule; nothing could be allowed to slip beneath his guard again.

But as she went on listing concerns he knew there were things he wouldn't change for her, the power-boat race amongst them. The arrival of the ambassador was something he could not have anticipated, and he regretted the way she'd lost her berth, but ambassadors, like kings, expected lesser mortals to make way for them, and this time Ellie had been in the way.

He explained this to her, but his excuses for an over-zealous agent sat awkwardly with him. The eviction notice was something he would have liked to handle himself, but the demands of a vast business empire meant he couldn't always be on the spot. He'd make it up to all the local men who'd been involved. And maybe to Ellie. Whatever she said, money would soften the blow. He reminded her that her new mooring would be available to her year-round at a peppercorn rent, adding, 'You should be able to start making a reasonable profit right away—'

'Profit?' she railed at him. 'Is that all you think about, Alexander?'

Someone had to, he thought wryly, wisely keeping those thoughts to himself. 'Of course not all the time, but you should think about profit if you want your business to be a long-term success...'

'I do think about it. I'm not a complete dunderhead, you know.'

He walked over to the sofa and sat down with her. She didn't flinch, which was a start. He had come to realise that she expected violence to erupt out of nothing and so took care not to trespass on her private space. 'I'm not suggesting you are.'

'Yes, well...' She moved away from him.

Beneath that steady gaze was a trembling little heart. He could crush her with ease, more easily than most; one rash move on his part and it would all be over, her passion, her determination, everything would melt beneath an avalanche of fear. Who had scarred her? He should demand to know. But that wasn't the best way with Ellie, he was learning. He didn't like this feeling of being shut out; he wasn't used to it. Everything was available to him, day or night. 'If you need any help with your business plan…'

'I'll employ a strategist,' she bit back at him sarcastically.

What was he doing now? Offering his services as a business consultant? The only thing he could be certain of where Ellie was concerned was that where a woman would shrink from violence, a man would confront it head-on, as he had done. He didn't like to think of her shrinking from anything; not Ellie. The fight in her was what made her so…adorable.

It was hard to believe she could relax for a moment with Alexander sitting close by. Normally the thought of being alone with a man was enough to make her rigid with fear. They were both holding things back, Ellie sensed, things that made them the people they were. You didn't reveal those things; those were the final boundaries that they would never have the chance to cross.

'Are you seriously asking me to believe you didn't know your men had chained off half the ocean?'

'Only half of it?' he said, angling his head to stare at her.

Did he have to do that? Humour was the one thing that defused her anger. It warmed every part of her too, which was a warning.

Alexander was staring at Ellie now in a way that was making her hot all over. The tug at one corner of his mouth was dangerously close to a smile…a smile that she was definitely tempted to respond to. To counter this crazy feeling she got up and started to pace the room. 'Those chains must be removed before someone has a serious accident.'

'I'll look into it,' he agreed.

'And your power-boat race is still going ahead?'

'It is.' He didn't need to yell about it and spoke quietly, reminding her that Alexander was absolute ruler of his world.

He unfolded from the sofa like some mythical warrior and came to stand in front of her to cut off her pacing square. Now she was staring at his dress studs, black diamonds cut to display their hard, cold surface to best advantage; how appropriate!

If Alexander thought he could intimidate her, he was probably right. She had been protected from conflict on the tiny island until he arrived, protected by the people who in the last and most crucial battle had let her down. They seemed to think he was a man they could deal with, while she…while she had a heart that was thundering so loud she could hardly hear herself think.

'Carving up oceans has never been part of my plan, and I will look into the dangers you mention,' Alexander said, moving towards the door.

Her interview was at an end; she had better make the most of the last few seconds remaining. 'There are submerged rocks where boats founder and men are lost—' Her voice choked off as she remembered the terrible night when her father had lost his life.

'I should be getting back to the party—'

'Of course…' She shook off the cold hand of the past.

'You should have more trust in me, Ellie.'

'Why should I?' She stared up at him. 'I don't even know you, none of us knows you. Who knows what kind of man you are?'

What kind of man was he? Good question! He had grown up on a neighbouring island, and had been a happy and contented fisherman until his bride had been lured away to Lefkis by Demetrios Lindos. He'd been poor then, of course, and Demetrios had been rich. He knew then that the only way to numb the pain and reclaim his honour was to be even richer, even more powerful than Demetrios. This return to Lefkis was his triumph. It should have been plain sailing. It would have been, had it not been for Ellie Mendoras.

He'd left the simple life behind years ago, and could look back now and see that he hadn't done so to get back at Demetrios, but to bury the devastation he had felt when his first love left him for another man. The sense of betrayal that had provoked had never left him. As his attention returned to Ellie his gaze fixed on the ugly scar. She had been wounded too; who knew how deeply? Reaching out, he did something that surprised him more than her. He touched her face. He brushed her hair back gently, exposing the scar. 'Who did this to you, Ellie?' he asked her gently.

Her answer was to press her lips together.

'Tell me—'

'Have you forgotten your party?'

He got the message. The subject of the scar and how she'd got it was firmly closed.

CHAPTER FIVE

ALEXANDER had seen the evidence of her fear, as well as her reaction to him, both of which would provoke his curiosity. But she would never tell him about the scar. She was used to people staring at it, particularly strangers, and she wasn't naïve enough to think they didn't draw their own conclusions. But no one had ever intruded to the point where they had asked her about it. No one, except for Alexander...

Her look had warned him to drop the subject. There was no way she could answer his question without revealing the truth, and she wasn't about to do that. She couldn't pass the scar off as nothing either. How could she when it affected every aspect of her life? It was a brand of shame she would always wear, and a cruel reminder that things were never as you wanted them to be.

Would she ever trust a man again? Ellie wondered as Alexander walked across the room. He came to a halt in front of one of the vast, panoramic windows and, gazing out across the twinkling lights and ghostly shapes that characterised the harbour at night, he said, 'I admire your ingenuity.'

'My...'

'Your uniform...' He turned around.

A faint smile touched Ellie's lips. 'I bartered with a local girl—'

'You bartered?'

Yes, bartered the gold chain her mother had given her, and for what? She had achieved nothing by it. Alexander was implacable; nothing could move him. 'It was nothing—' She brushed it off; she didn't want to get into it.

'Nothing?' he pressed.

'Shouldn't you be getting back to your guests?' She glanced at the door.

'You're giving up again,' Alexander murmured in a soft tone that made her heart race.

'No, I'm not. Not even for a moment.' She waved her arm in frustration; unfortunately, her defiant gesture sent a vase flying. Alexander caught it and returned it to its stand.

'Perhaps a glass of champagne would steady your nerves,' he suggested, locking eyes with her.

'My nerves are fine.'

He didn't answer this assertion; he didn't need to.

Her hand was on the door handle. She should just leave. But was she in such a hurry because she couldn't trust Alexander, or because she couldn't trust herself? Ellie wondered.

She gave a shocked exclamation as he touched her scar.

'If someone on Lefkis did this to you, I should know—'

'How it happened is none of your business, Alexander.' Ellie willed her voice to remain steady as she attempted to stare him out.

'What if I make it my business?'

'Please don't…' She averted her face. 'Please let me go… Luigi will be waiting for me—'

'Damn Luigi!'

'He needs me. The ship is packed with your guests, Alexander. I can't let him down.'

'You're going to go out there and work as a waitress?'

'What's wrong with that?' Ellie held her head high, daring Alexander to say another word. 'Everything I possess in this world I have earned—'

'I don't doubt it,' he murmured.

'It might not seem much to you, but there are things in life that matter more to me than money—'

'Such as?'

The breath hitched in Ellie's throat as Alexander moved closer. A moment ago she would have been able to give him a list of things, but now…now all she was aware of was the electricity shooting between them. If he knew the truth about her he would despise her just as her late mother's elderly friend had promised her every man would.

The list of charges against her was growing like weeds in Ellie's mind. It wasn't as if the old man who had attacked her had a history of violence, or sexual assault… 'Who would believe a young girl hadn't led a wealthy old man on?'

She could still hear his rasping voice beating every shred of self-belief out of her. 'Who would believe the scar on her cheek was anything more than the result of an unfortunate accident? He was so old his hands trembled, did they? Look!' he had said, thrusting them out in front of her. 'Could he force a young and healthy girl to do anything she didn't want to do?'

Realising Alexander was staring at her, Ellie pulled her hand away from her face. The old man had assaulted many other young girls, she had discovered subsequently, but he had never been brought to book. He had informed her that no man would enjoy her after him; he had said this dispassionately just before he ground out the glowing butt of his cigar on her face. She had passed out from the pain and had woken to find him panting and damp beside her like a spent jellyfish...

'You look like you could use this more than champagne...'

Ellie stared in bewilderment as Alexander pressed a glass of ice-cold water into her hand as slowly she came round. Neither she nor any of the other girls the old man had assaulted had been to blame, Ellie realised in a blinding flash of understanding. The only reason he had never been brought to justice was that there wasn't an official he couldn't bribe. 'Thank you...' She nursed the glass, avoiding Alexander's gaze. He must not suspect what was on her mind.

'Are you thinking about something in the past, Ellie?'

Could he read her mind? She flared a glance at him, and in that instant she saw an answering something that made her ache for him. She wasn't the only one who had suffered pain in the past. It made her want to reach out to him. That, and the fact that wealth could be used as a weapon for good or evil... 'Alexander, I've got an idea.'

He pulled his hand away and stepped back. If he stayed that close to her any longer they wouldn't be going anywhere but to bed.

'Please listen to me, Alexander—'

He didn't have any intention of listening to her crazy schemes. 'I've done that, and you should know by now that I never change any of my plans on a whim.'

'I'm not asking you to.'

'I need hard proof before anything changes—'

'Then let me give you some,' she said eagerly.

'How?' He frowned, wondering what was coming next.

'Come out with me. Come out with me on my boat, Alexander.'

'Alone?' He couldn't resist it. His lips curved in a mocking smile.

'You'll be quite safe,' she promised him with matching irony.

He felt a rush of arousal as they started sparring again. She made him feel alive. Forgetting the haunting fears had made her eyes glow bright. She was changing, maturing, gaining in confidence; she was not afraid to seize the moment, and she refused to be defeated or downhearted. He might find the transformation irresistible, but this time he would have to disappoint her. 'It's a nice thought, Ellie, and I thank you for the invitation, but unfortunately I don't have time…'

For the island, for the people and for her, Ellie gathered. What had she been thinking? She could see how ridiculous her suggestion must have sounded now. Why would Alexander Kosta waste his time on one of her tourist trips? Just because she took such pride in them didn't mean they could interest a man who had the world and all its treasures at his beck and call.

But try as she might Ellie could think of no better way to show Alexander exactly what was at risk, and how easily the delicate balance of ocean life could be destroyed if the wrong route was chosen for the race.

'Would you like me to have someone guide you into port and show you your new mooring?' he said, clearly believing the subject was closed.

'No, thank you, I can manage,' Ellie answered distractedly. 'I'm sure the harbour master will direct me when I arrive…'

'Whatever charges you incur you will be compensated—'

'Compensated?' That did it! 'You've got no idea, have you?' Ellie raged, turning the full blaze of her emerald-green eyes on Alexander.

'What do you mean?' he said.

'You're heartless! Heartless and cruel!' she blazed at him. 'I wonder when exactly you stopped caring—or were you just born this way? You've paid your money over, and now you think that's the end of it?' she demanded incredulously.

'It should be—'

'You could do more; so much more,' she declared passionately.

'Such as?'

'Such as taking the trouble to go down to the new moorings—'

'Why would I want to do that?'

Ellie huffed with exasperation and rolled her eyes. 'So you can make sure everyone's happy and have everything they need, maybe?'

He had an army of staff to do things like that for him. 'I'll see what I can do—'

'No, Alexander, I want more than that—'

'What? What do you want from me, Ellie?' He was losing that famous self-control of his again.

'I want your promise, Alexander. I want a commitment from you.'

He looked at her again just to be sure he'd heard her correctly. 'Are you telling me what to do?'

'I'm asking you,' she said firmly, holding his gaze.

'I have a diary to consult—'

'And appointments that can be changed, I presume?'

No one had ever spoken to him like this before. No one ever questioned his judgement. The way she was firming her lips with determination had drawn his attention to them when that was the last thing on earth he needed right now. 'You have my word,' he said. 'I promise I will see what I can do.' And with that she must be satisfied, Alexander thought, staring at Ellie's mouth.

'When? When are you coming to the harbour, Alexander?'

His natural reaction was to come down hard on her. He should be ordering her, warning her, winding up the pressure until she backed down. But as she continued to stare boldly at him he started wondering what it would cost him to pay a visit to the harbour. The thought of mixing with the fishermen, listening to their concerns, hearing their stories, took him right back to his days at sea...

More than that, his body was agreeing readily to the idea of seeing Ellie again; it wasn't easy to be objective with her fresh, clean scent rolling over him. There were many ways this evening could end and letting her go didn't seem to be one of them. He had to admit this confrontation was such a novelty for him he'd have to be numb from the neck down not to wonder how Ellie's defiance and passion would translate in bed.

'This is so good of you, Alexander,' she said with confidence before he'd even made his final decision. 'I know the fishermen and their families would really appreciate it. I want to thank you on their behalf—'

'I haven't said I'm coming yet,' he reminded her.

'But you will. I know you will, and I know you'll enjoy going out on a real boat for a change...'

'Hmm, a real boat,' he said, as if such a thing were completely new for him.

The worst of it was she was right—he would enjoy going out on a real boat again. 'OK, you've closed the deal; now back off,' he warned. He could already feel the resistance of raw wood beneath his naked feet. To feel a fishing smack pitch and yaw as he coaxed its curmudgeonly workings to respond was a temptation he couldn't resist. She'd made that possible for him. Ellie had managed to find his Achilles' heel, the one thing that would make him bend a little. He'd seen her boat, glimpsed it, glanced at it, tried to ignore it and failed. It was part of that untidy side of the island he had intended to change, but in spite of his determination to do so her old boat had planted a seed of longing in his heart that he simply hadn't been able to shake off. It was a longing to return to those less complicated days when he had believed that anything was possible, and that he could make it so. But in those days he had also believed that love would last forever, Alexander reminded himself, hardening his heart again.

'You still haven't told me when to expect you,' she pressed, staring up at him.

'I'll let you know.' He firmed his jaw. He was still awash with memories—man against the sea, man against the elements, man yearning for release. In spite of his massive wealth that primitive part of him had remained largely unsatisfied, Alexander realised.

'But you will come?'

He made a sound of exasperation, but as he refocused on Ellie he suddenly realised how tired she looked. 'Yes, I'll come,' he said. He had to admit it had taken wit and courage for her to come here and confront him, and he knew she would keep right on until he finally agreed. Normally, that was a sign for him to tighten the screws and win the battle, but in this case it wasn't that easy. Ellie wasn't frightened of him— at least, not in the way he'd first thought. She wasn't overawed by Alexander Kosta the Greek tycoon, but she was very frightened indeed of Alexander Kosta the man. It was his strength, his physical strength, the very thing he had been rejoicing in only moments ago that put the guardedness back in her eyes.

What did he expect? This was a woman who had been physically scarred by some monster. Did he expect her to react normally when she was alone with a man? It made him all the more determined to find out how it had happened, and who had done it to her, but first he was going to get rid of that fear in her eyes. 'Damn the party!' he said softly, leaning past her to close the door.

CHAPTER SIX

AS THEIR eyes locked Ellie was still coming to terms with the fact that Alexander had agreed to visit the harbour and speak to the men. It meant so much to her she was still starry-eyed. But the way Alexander was staring at her now was deeply disquieting.

'Don't turn your head,' he said. Cupping her chin, he brought her back to face him. She forced herself to hold his gaze.

'I don't want you to be afraid, Ellie—'

'I'm not afraid,' she argued hotly. But inside she was, and Alexander knew it. She was afraid of the way he made her feel. She would never forget his kiss, or how it felt to be wrapped in his arms. The memory was like oxygen to the fear inside her as well as to the fire spreading through her veins. Reason told her to back away, to get out of here before it was too late, while every nerve-ending argued fiercely that she must stay. 'I should go,' she protested weakly. 'My duties—'

'I have explained your absence to Luigi.'

'You have?' As Ellie's brain snapped into focus again she pulled away. Alexander made no attempt to bring her back into his embrace. For a moment she stood undecided as to what to do.

'I said you were needed elsewhere,' he said, watching her

with barely concealed amusement. 'But if you want to go…'
He shrugged.

Ellie tipped her chin. 'Of course I want to go. I don't take
on a job and leave it half-undone—'

'That's my way too,' Alexander assured her, dragging
her to him.

She should have resisted him, of course she should, but
why would she want to put steel back into bones that were
melting into honey? Why should she fight him when she
trusted him to hold her and keep her safe? And trusting him,
why shouldn't she kiss him back?

Lacing her fingers through his hair to keep him close, Ellie
shuddered with arousal. She was finding out again how well
they fitted together. How could that be possible? Alexander
was so big and she was so small, and yet every contour, every
super-sensitised part of her seemed to connect with him, and
meld with him. This moment, this feeling, this freedom,
wasn't something to be frightened of, it was something to
embrace; the future and all it held could wait for another day.
At that moment she felt a freedom she'd never let herself experience before. A freedom free of fear. She stared shyly into
his eyes. 'You don't frighten me, Alexander…'

Sweeping her into his arms, Alexander managed to gather
up the ice bucket before he left the room. He carried her into
his bedroom and laid her down on the bed. Her senses were
heightened; she took in everything…the scent of cool, clean
linen, and the fan whirring overhead. The big bed with its firm
mattress, and the tingling sensation of having Alexander
stretched out beside her; protector, not predator; a lover and
not an aggressive male. Tentatively she reached for him. The
truth was she wanted him…

As Alexander sat up to tug off his shirt Ellie rolled onto

her back to watch him undress. It was something she could never have imagined herself doing. Letting go of the past had always seemed such an impossible dream. Yet now all she could think of was pressing every part of her against Alexander, testing his strength, feeling the warmth of his naked skin against her own.

He stood for a moment like a bronze statue. He reminded her of a gladiator in some ancient etching. His chest and arms were banded with muscle and shaded with dark hair…hair that dipped into a V before disappearing beneath the leather belt cinching his waist. She wanted to experience what it would be like to have those hard muscles pressing into her, and she wanted to feel that chest hair rasping her nipples. She wanted teasing, stroking; she wanted all of it. He smiled when she moved her legs restlessly on the bed.

'Would you like a drink, or some ice to cool you down?'

'I don't know what you mean.' Except her voice might just have betrayed her with its huskiness…

'I think ice,' Alexander decided.

Ellie gasped. Before she had chance to say no Alexander had scooped up a handful of ice cubes from the ice bucket by the bed and had pressed them against the pulse throbbing hectically at the side of her neck. 'This should calm you down,' he said, resisting her attempt to push him away.

'Alexander, I can't bear it…'

'Pity, when there's worse to come…'

'There is?' she said shyly. Far from calming her down, the sensation of ice against her heated skin had only stirred her senses to a new fever pitch.

Taking some ice into his mouth, he kissed her deeply. Heat shot through her. Opening her blouse he grabbed another handful and pressed it against her breasts. She gasped and bucked towards him.

'Shall I warm you?' Alexander suggested innocently.

She gave a little cry as his mouth closed over one tender nipple. The ice had made her more than sensitive, and while she was still whimpering and writhing on the bed he repeated the treatment with her other breast. She was on fire for him, and she was freezing. She was laughing, and gasping with shock. She was pushing him away, and begging for more…much more.

'You have beautiful breasts,' he said, holding on the delicious torture to give himself chance to admire the effect.

'Don't stop…please, please, please don't stop…' That was as much as she could manage; she dared not interrupt him. But even through the miasma of pleasure she was able to accept and enjoy the compliment. She had never thought any part of her beautiful before, and she still didn't, but just for that one brief moment Alexander had made her feel as though she might be.

'More?' he said, reaching into the ice bucket. She gasped as he pushed her skirt down and teased her belly with yet more ice cubes. The liquid was running down her legs and teasing places he mustn't guess. Fortunately he was busy lapping the water up, though the heat of his tongue and the chill of the ice was proving to be a sensational combination, and she didn't know how long she could hide the extent of her arousal from him. The more ice he held against her the more the fires inside her raged. She wanted him, she craved release, she wanted free of all her clothes…

Taking an ice cube in his mouth, he kissed her hard. She was filled with the delicious scent and taste of him…on ice; the most delicious cocktail ever invented. And now he was moving down the bed, dropping icy kisses everywhere...on her thighs, on her belly, always missing the place she wanted him to be. 'How can you be so cruel?' she managed somehow to gasp out.

'Quite easily,' he said, levelling one of his sardonic gazes on her face.

Tiny shock waves of anticipation were already spreading through her.

'You're driving me crazy, making me want you like this,' Alexander informed her, licking her belly again. As he circled her navel with his tongue she could feel an answering sensation between her thighs.

Bucking shamelessly towards him, she begged him for more, and while she did that she was helping him to discard the rest of their clothes. Then somehow one of her legs became lodged over Alexander's shoulder and she cried out with excitement again as he began using the ice in the most extraordinary places. When he replaced the ice with his firm lips, tongue and knowing fingers it was almost all over. But he knew, and drew back, making her wait for him to touch her where she was aching to be touched. And then he did at last, stroking her delicately, rhythmically, as he skilfully interpreted her every wanton thought.

Ellie called out Alexander's name in an urgent whisper as her excitement grew. The powerful column of his neck, the wide spread of his shoulders...muscle and sinew clearly delineated, moving on to a flat stomach with abdominal muscles flexed and hard. She wanted him so badly it was like a pain growing inside her that she knew only he could ease. Her body yearned for him, her soul ached for him, and as he nudged her thighs apart...

She stopped him.

'I can't do this, Alexander…'

He might have called to her, or reached for her, Ellie had no idea. Rolling off the bed, she snatched up her clothes and fled.

As she backed away from him and he saw those wide, frightened eyes he didn't fight her decision to leave. She made him think of a young and vulnerable rabbit bolting when you least expected it to.

He remained where he was, motionless on the bed. He listened to the sound of her dressing in the bathroom and then to her running feet until he couldn't hear them any more. He was filled with so many thoughts he could hardly pick them apart to examine them one by one. All he knew was he had been wrong about Ellie. Whatever had frightened her wasn't as bad as he had thought; it was worse.

CHAPTER SEVEN

HE SHOULD have followed her. He didn't like loose ends, or loose cannons, but the ambassador was one of his guests tonight, which left him staring over the side of the yacht at a small red inflatable captained by a girl whose determined profile told him that at least she had recovered, and for that he was relieved.

Not only had she recovered, but Ellie had also fulfilled all her duties to Luigi before leaving the yacht, and she had done that with a composure that had astounded him. After the way she had fled he had imagined she would run straight off the boat. Far from it. She had reported for duty, and then acted out the part of waitress as if she couldn't hear the gossip surrounding her. She had been one of the last to leave and had waited until Luigi had given her permission to go.

He'd watched her as she moved about his guests, discreetly serving them and remaining calm when they were rude to her, as people so often were to staff when they'd had a drink. He'd barely been able to focus on what the ambassador was saying to him while his thoughts were awash with Ellie, and his desire to defend her. The look she'd given him had been enough to change his mind about that.

He pushed back from the rail at last. He had to be sure she

was safe before he could turn away. She had some hold on the local people's hearts he couldn't understand. She was only half Greek, for instance, and this was a very conservative island. Her English mother had run back to the safety of her middle-class roots, deserting her Greek fisherman. Surely that was enough to turn the people against Ellie? But plainly not. If the mother had found the gulf between fantasy and reality too great it was clear the daughter must have been drawn by the ocean; it could do that. The elders of the island, having watched and assessed Ellie in their quiet and shrewd way, had come to accept her as one of their own. Even so, he couldn't allow her to stand in his way, or turn his people against him.

Before leaving the deck he called to one of his men. 'Be sure to lay illuminated marker buoys around that fishing boat...' He pointed out Ellie's boat. He couldn't risk an accident in the dark. 'And then make sure that my *Fairline*'s fuelled and ready for the morning...'

The man saluted him and then went silently about his business. Ellie might have run away from him, and then acted out a part for the rest of the evening, but he had no intention of leaving things here.

Could she curl up any smaller? Was she trying to disappear? The fishing boat was swaying gently but, even lulled by the soporific rhythms of the tide, Ellie couldn't relax. Usually all she had to do was let her mind wander through the busy sea world beneath her bunk and count the fishes to fall asleep. But not tonight; tonight nothing worked for her. She felt as if there were as many challenges in her world as there were fish in the sea.

Which explained why she was dressed for the Arctic rather

than a warm Greek night! Her winter pyjamas had elasticised wrists and ankles, which meant she felt safe, shapeless and sexless—mainly safe. It was the best way to be.

She was wearing armour to protect her from Alexander Kosta, Ellie thought, sitting up in bed. She couldn't keep him out of her thoughts however hard she tried to. And now it was three o'clock in the morning, Ellie realised, grimacing. All the lights had been dimmed on board the *Olympus*… All but one set. Alexander never slept. Instead he must think, plan and prowl his way through the night. The one thing she could never imagine was Alexander sleeping like a baby—

And why was she thinking about him at all?

Crawling back under the covers, Ellie turned her face into the pillows. It was time for counting fishes.

The wind was soft on Ellie face as she sailed into the new harbour. The journey had been easy, the sea mirror-smooth and silver-coloured tinged with pink in the thin early-morning light. There were deeper pewter shadows below the horizon, but the sky was a clear, safe turquoise that promised fair weather for the rest of the day.

As she made the final turn into the harbour and began to cruise slowly into port she saw a sight that had her biting her lip to hold back tears. Far from needing the harbour master, or one of Alexander's men to guide her in, all the fishermen and their families had all come down to the quay to welcome her to her new home.

As she waved some of the women started throwing flowers into the sea in anticipation of her arrival. It was the traditional greeting in Lefkis for a sailor who had returned after a long voyage. Which in fact she had taken in so many ways, Ellie reflected.

This was what she was fighting for, Ellie thought as she flung a mooring line to one of the waiting men. This was why she could never leave Lefkis, even though she had Alexander to contend with.

She only had to blink and he was in her mind again, Ellie realised impatiently. Try as she might she couldn't stop dreaming about him, and the only consolation was that dreams were safe.

Ellie thought about Alexander later as she went about the boat, cleaning and preparing everything in readiness for her tour. It was due to depart at noon. Even with that distraction she managed to finish her work on time, and stood with her hands on her hips to survey her handiwork. Each piece of brass on board her boat gleamed, and every bit of deck had been swept, scrubbed and oiled until the old planks felt like silk beneath her naked feet. Everything was ready for the tour, and now she just had to hope that her passengers would find their way to the new berth without difficulty.

The tinge of anxiety Ellie was feeling yielded to hunger. The scent of food was floating up to her from one of the harbour-side cafés. It didn't take much for her mouth to water as she imagined the pastries and coffee, and freshly squeezed juice...

Ellie chose a café where the fishermen and their families usually congregated. She found everyone in high spirits. They greeted her warmly. Perhaps she had misread the fishermen's feelings about their new port, Ellie conceded. All the men assured her they were delighted, and particularly with the peppercorn rent.

So, Alexander wasn't a monster—at least where the fisher-men were concerned. The new harbour would suit them better in the summer months, the men told her, as they were closer to the seasonal fishing ground. Plus, it turned out that Alexander had assured them they would be moving back to

the shelter of the deep-water harbour for the winter season.
When there wouldn't be any visiting tourists, Ellie assumed,
though, in fairness, what they'd told her showed Alexander
in a good light.

So why hadn't he told her that? What did he get out of
winding her up? Deciding not to think too deeply about it she
placed her order for breakfast.

As she ate she thought about what she'd learned. It made
sense that the historic home of the fishing fleet was on the
other side of the island, because that had been the first side
to be developed, but now there were equal services all over
Lefkis. The proximity to their fishing ground was good news
for the fishermen, but her concerns about the power-boat
racing still held. If the wrong route was chosen for that there
could still be an ecological disaster.

She had to hurry up, though it was hard to rush such delicious food. The orange juice was squeezed in front of her, and
the pastries came hot and fresh from the oven. The coffee was
poured out inky black, but then at least an inch of cream had
been added, into which for good measure she stirred a
spoonful of the delectable Greek honey.

Flexing her naked feet with contentment, Ellie was just
settling into her second pastry when out of the corner of her
eye she caught sight of a man dipping his head to come into
the café. Her heart stopped beating. She turned away. That
didn't help when she could feel him behind her. He had
paused just inside the café, she suspected, and now he was
looking around.

Her hands had started shaking, Ellie realised. The meal she
had been enjoying was definitely over; she wouldn't get
another thing past the fist in her throat. Drawing in a deep
breath, she swivelled around on her stool.

How could she have mistaken this man for Alexander?

Ellie had been so certain it was Alexander walking into the café it was a shock to be confronted by a man she didn't know.

'Ms Mendoras?'

'That's right.'

'I have a letter for you.'

Ellie reached out to take the envelope. The man was wearing the uniform of Alexander's crew and the square of thick cream vellum looked like an invitation. If only her heart would stop hammering so she might be able to breathe properly and concentrate. Seeing the bold handwriting didn't help.

'I have been instructed to wait for your reply, Ms Mendoras.'

What was Alexander playing at now? With a faint smile at his crew member Ellie turned away to find out.

As a verbal invitation hadn't worked last time, he was formally inviting her to dine on board the *Olympus* that evening. It was an opportunity for her to meet and talk to the oceanographers he'd hired to help him plan the route of the power-boat race, the note went on. Conscious of the man waiting for her answer, Ellie skim-read the rest of it—something about reassurance, and loose ends to tie up…

Loose ends? Ellie blenched. How would she face Alexander after last night?

Quite simply by attending his dinner, she concluded. Did she want him to think he had frightened her off? Would she get another chance to air her concerns about the power-boat racing if she didn't go?

Fixing a polite smile to her face, she turned around. 'Please inform Kirie Kosta that I will be pleased to attend his dinner party this evening. Eight o'clock on board the *Olympus*?' Ellie waited and received a curt nod in reply. Turning back to her breakfast, she toyed with some crumbs and then put her knife down again. What had she done now? She had nothing to wear—nothing that was suitable for dinner on board the *Olympus*, at least.

So she would find something, Ellie determined, wiping her hands on her oil-stained dungarees. She was so busy wondering how she was going to do that with a tour going out at noon she nearly shot off her stool when someone touched her lightly on the shoulder.

'I didn't mean to startle you—'

'Alexander!' He did mean to startle her; she was sure of that much. And now she had to try and appear nonchalant—though admittedly that wasn't easy while she was clutching her throat.

She couldn't remember ever having seen him dressed so casually. She would *definitely* have remembered!

'I wasn't sure you'd be here—'

'And I was sure you wouldn't be here,' Ellie countered smartly, recovering.

'I must apologise for interrupting your breakfast...'

But his lips were tugging down in a way that made him look wholly unrepentant. And why was she staring at his lips? 'You didn't spoil my breakfast. I'd just finished, as it happens.' Slipping down from her stool, she tried to move past him. 'Excuse me, please...'

'Not so fast...'

She had to get a grip. She didn't want a rerun of last night. She stood her ground stubbornly until Alexander was forced to move to one side.

'So,' he said, 'are you coming tonight?'

'I've already told your messenger that I am. Thank you,' she added belatedly, gazing past him.

'I mustn't keep you...' Thankfully, he took the hint and moved aside.

Ellie's heart was thundering as she searched through her pocket for some money to pay for breakfast.

'Let me pay,' Alexander offered, guessing what she was up to.

Ellie finally managed to locate some scrunched-up euro notes. She brandished them with relief. 'No need...' Moving in front of Alexander, she made sure to reach the cashier before him. She didn't want to be beholden to Alexander Kosta for a single cent. However many cronies he might have coming to his dinner party tonight, she wasn't one of them.

'No, your breakfast is on the house,' the café owner insisted, waving Ellie's money away. 'This is my treat today to welcome you to your new home. We think a lot of this girl on Lefkis,' he told Alexander.

The café owner's kindly brown eyes twinkled at Ellie as she laughed with embarrassment. 'You don't have to do this,' she assured him. 'If any of your young relatives would like a trip out on my boat one day—'

'All twenty-nine of them?' He spread his arms wide and laughed.

'Several trips,' Ellie amended, starting to smile. 'And now, if you'll excuse me?' Her voice sharpened as she turned to look at Alexander.

'Of course...' He gave her a mocking bow as she went past him.

Did everything that man did have to make her quiver? Ellie stopped to drag in a deep, refreshing breath as she stepped outside, and checked her hands to see if they really were trembling as badly as she thought. Alexander! That man was—

'Such a hero...'

Ellie turned to see a group of local women gazing rapturously at him. That was all she needed. Alexander, plus fan club! His arrogance would just grow and grow!

'Can't you delay your tour to enjoy the celebrations?' he asked her, keeping in step.

'Celebrations?' Ellie said suspiciously.

'It's just a few drinks down on the quay. I want to make sure everyone's happy with the new arrangements. It's a shame if you can't join us, seeing as you suggested it.'

Dig! Dig! Dig! 'I have a tour leaving at midday, so I'm afraid I won't be able to join you.'

'Never mind. We'll make up for it tonight…'

We will? Ellie gulped. Secretly, that was what she was afraid of. There were quite a few *loose ends* to tie up now she came to think about it. 'I'll see you at dinner,' she said, already regretting her agreement to go.

'I'm looking forward to it…'

I'm sure you are, Ellie thought, wondering what she had agreed to let herself in for.

She had nothing to wear. Absolutely nothing. This wasn't a joke, it was a full-blown disaster. How was she supposed to convince people to take her seriously while they would all be in evening clothes, and she was wearing oil-stained rags?

Of course she could always turn up in shorts and a sun top, Ellie reasoned drily. If she were completely mad, that was. So her selection consisted of faded tops, oil-stained shorts and a nice new pair of dungarees.

Perfect.

Throwing all the clothes down on her bunk, Ellie asked herself why she had ever agreed to Alexander's dinner invitation. She didn't go out to dinner. She didn't go out anywhere. Why would it occur to her to have clothes suitable for eating dinner on a billionaire's yacht?

She'd had the most wonderful tour that day with a boat full of enthusiastic people and was already fully booked for the next trip. Fantastic! Brilliant! Except her main concern right now was the effect the power-boat races would have on the ocean. There might not be any more tours if Alexander and his people chose the wrong route, which meant she had to go to his wretched dinner even if she had to sew tea towels into a toga.

With only an hour left to go Ellie was still undecided what to wear. Plus her hair, which needed oodles of attention after a day at sea, was bundled up in a towel after her shower. Appearance was everything when it came to selling your point of view. She'd learned that much at the council chamber on Sunday, and, however much she cared, no one, especially the type of eminent professors Alexander would no doubt have lined up, would want to spend time with someone who looked like a tramp.

She had to do something, and soon...

Frowning as she gazed out of the porthole, Ellie suddenly sprang to life. Racing up the companionway, she ran across the deck and hung over the rail, waving her arms frantically. She was wearing the latest in a long line of outfits to have failed the test—an ugly, oversized shirt, tucked into faded black trousers. In all honesty, it did not a sophisticated dinner outfit make, but now she had one final chance to save the day.

Yelling as loud as she could, Ellie gasped with relief when she managed to catch the attention of the young waitress who had helped her out the previous evening.

CHAPTER EIGHT

'CAN you help me?' It seemed such an impossible task, and Ellie hardly liked to ask the girl to help her again. She was so beautiful, for one thing, tall and slim, with dark, flashing eyes and a mass of gleaming ebony hair cascading down her back. Her nose was neat, her brows effortlessly plucked, and her skin was flawless...

And she was touching the ugly scar on her cheek, until the young girl took hold of her hand and gently drew it away.

'Of course I can help you...' Holding Ellie's gaze, she squeezed her hand.

'I'm afraid I don't have anything else to give you.' Ellie thought it only fair to point this out at the start. She made sure not to let her gaze wander to her mother's chain glinting on the girl's olive skin.

'I don't want anything from you,' the young girl assured her. Catching hold of Ellie's hand, she gave her a look that was both warm and teasing. 'Come on, let's get started; it will be fun...'

Fun? Thinking about Alexander was a lot of things, but fun wasn't one of them, but now she'd started down this path she had to carry on.

* * *

'Well, what do you think?' The young girl Ellie had befriended was asking her friends and family, who had all clustered into the tiny bedroom to admire the result of her handiwork.

To Ellie's relief the response was unanimously positive. Maybe her idea wasn't such a bad one, after all. The women were dressed in traditional costume for the special holiday Alexander had declared, but they had dressed Ellie in a fabulous slinky dress and a pair of stratospherically high heels. She had never worn anything remotely glamorous in her life before, but now she felt like Cinderella after a visit by a whole host of fairy godmothers.

The excitement was growing to fever pitch in the small room. Alexander had organised fireworks on the pier and stalls for the children with sweets and ice cream. Everywhere was lit up and decorated with streamers, and later there would be music so the men could dance the proud, strong dances of Lefkis… And here was the woman who had received a personal invitation from the man himself.

And she was shaking! And not hiding it very well.

'And what do you think of yourself, Ellie?'

Ellie hardly knew how to reply as she stared into the full-length mirror the women had propped up. She hugged her new young friend instead.

What *did* she think? Wow! Er, gosh! Ellie smoothed the shiny red satin bodice and looked at herself critically in the mirror. She was hardly qualified to judge. Her knowledge of fashion was so limited. It was certainly a different look from a boiler suit or shorts. The slinky gown was sculpted to her breasts and made her waist seem tiny. The front was low-cut and exposed her breasts. They were full breasts; she had almost forgotten how full. And they didn't look bad, tanned as they were to an even, honey-coloured sheen. And her hips…where had they come from? The dress moulded her buttocks, making them a sexual statement, rather than something comfortable to sit on.

'I think the dress is absolutely beautiful,' she said honestly—she just wasn't sure about herself in it. 'I don't know how to thank you for lending it to me.' As Ellie turned full circle everyone laughed happily and clapped their hands in approval.

They even managed to tame her hair before she left them, pinning it up at the sides, and finishing the tumbling mass of auburn curls with bold silk flowers. Ellie didn't even care that the hairstyle revealed her scar. Why should she when no one else seemed concerned?

The girls had helped her with make-up, and their last touch was a spritz of scent. Looking in the mirror was like seeing a different person staring back.

Ellie lost confidence for a moment. She looked so like those other women who fawned over Alexander. And she was nothing like them. But she couldn't do anything about it now; she wouldn't dream of causing offence when everyone had gone to so much trouble.

'Your father would be very proud of you,' one of the young girls called out when she finally took the plunge and left. 'Just be happy, Ellie…'

A steward in a smart white dress uniform escorted Ellie to the door of the dining room. From there she was to enter the dining room alone. As he was about to swing the double doors open she asked him to wait for a moment. She needed a second to catch her breath. Coming on board the *Olympus* alone was an ordeal at any time. She always felt as if she was leaving the known territory of the shore behind and entering another kingdom. 'Thank you,' she said at last, managing a faint smile before tilting her chin up and walking in.

For a moment Ellie was blinded by the lights. Chandeliers were blazing down on her and there were candles flickering on the table. It took her a few seconds to realise that it was a very big dinner table indeed, and that the large gathering was incredibly formal, with everyone in evening dress. Why had she thought it would be a small, intimate group of people—just a few scientists, wasn't that what Alexander had said?

He hadn't actually told her anything other than the fact that there would be scientists present, Ellie remembered, feeling totally ridiculous as everyone turned to stare at her. She was way out of her comfort zone, and wearing clothes she was quite unaccustomed to. She felt ridiculous suddenly, naked and unsure of herself, and to make matters worse the animated conversation that had greeted her at the door had died completely.

At the head of the table at the far end of the room one man stood alone. Alexander looked splendidly imposing. There were women on either side of him, beautiful women, women whose gowns told Ellie in an instant that her dress was a copy and that theirs were the real thing. Perversely, it gave her courage. She couldn't have been more proud to be drawn into the young girl's home, where she had been the recipient of so much generosity.

The women were staring at her... Let them stare.

And now their elegantly painted lips were quirking with amusement... Their loss.

Firming her jaw, Ellie stood tall.

'Ellie...' Alexander's rich baritone captured everyone's attention. 'Ladies and gentlemen, may I present Ellie Mendoras...'

She was supposed to walk up to him, Ellie realised. Alexander was standing waiting for her. Did he want her to suffer the humiliation of walking the full length of the table with everyone staring at her?

So be it. She had already decided that that was what she was going to do.

Tilting her chin at a defiant angle, she started forward.

He was bowled over. Ellie's entrance into the room had completely stunned him. She was stunning. She was the most desirable woman he'd ever seen. Whatever he'd thought about her before went out the window. Where had she been hiding herself? Why…?

Never mind that now… Lust propelled him to his feet. Lust made him smile in sheer, undiluted admiration. His discerning gaze took in the voluptuous body and smooth, tanned skin. Her hair cascaded down her naked back in a way that made him want to lace his fingers through it and bring her head back to kiss her neck…

She was dreaming of humiliation—and then only briefly. Alexander must have come to her side within seconds of her entering the room, Ellie realised. She'd only been standing there by herself for a moment before he came to her, though it seemed like an hour with all those condemnatory stares resting on her face. And now, quite incredibly, he was offering to lead her to her place…

'Ellie…' Gazing down at her, Alexander offered her his arm as if she was his valued guest. She could hardly take it in, and had to be told twice to take her place, which she realised now was closest to the door, and a long way from Alexander.

'I'm sure you will enjoy the company of two of our most eminent professors,' he said, waving the waiters away so he could pull out the chair for her himself.

Ellie felt a *frisson* down her spine as Alexander moved close enough to settle her. And even when he pulled away and had returned to his place at the head of the table she was still trembling.

It was a relief to find that Alexander's social skills were such that the conversation around the table started up again almost immediately. Naturally, no one wanted to be thought unsophisticated by their host. If Alexander Kosta wished to entertain a local girl—a waitress, and some sort of activist, Ellie heard some of them murmuring—well, he set the tone, and they must be content. But a palpable air of drama had swept the proceedings as everyone waited to see what would happen next.

Ellie found herself seated between a man and a woman she knew by repute. Alexander hadn't been exaggerating when he'd said that he had invited the top scientists in the world to offer their advice on the best route for the power-boat race, and she had the added reassurance of knowing that people like these could not be bought.

Ellie found herself relaxing gradually, and she soon forgot the barbed comments and cruel stares. After all, designer gowns were the furthest thing from her mind now. She was in her element and too engrossed in conversation to concern herself with fashion. As that conversation progressed she looked at Alexander in a whole different way. In fact she looked at him lots of times, hoping he might look back at her. She'd like to show him she realised now he wasn't the monster she'd first thought him, but a deeply caring individual who had put conservation at the top of his agenda.

That wasn't enough, Ellie admitted to herself. With this new understanding of him she wanted Alexander to look at her as he'd looked at her when he stood by her side before leading her to her place at the table. That look had scorched the fear of men right out of her, and opened up a whole new world of possibilities.

Possibilities that must remain closed to her. Was she losing it completely?

Probably, Ellie conceded, watching Alexander drop some comment in the ear of the woman next to him; she felt like scratching her eyes out.

The brief encounter drew a whole world of mixed emotions from Ellie, not least of which was a fascination with the woman's flirting techniques. It looked as if you had to respond with a feline smile and half-closed eyes. This was a whole new language of sophisticated seduction, of which she had previously been totally unaware, and for which she clearly needed to brush up her skills.

Excusing herself from the table, Ellie sought refuge in the ladies' room to think things through. She really should apologise to Alexander for misjudging him. Great excuse for some one-on-one communication, but not foolproof… She could hardly ask to see him in private after their previous encounters. She wanted to take things more slowly this time—have time to savour the moment. Ellie was still working out her tactics when she heard the outer door to the ladies' room open. The laugher was growing closer. She was about to be cornered by some of Alexander's most sophisticated guests. Solution? Take cover in a cubicle until they left.

It only took a second or two in the enclosed space for Ellie to realise that she smelled of mothballs. It only took a moment longer than that to realise that the laughter behind the door was directed at Mothball Ellie, as they called her, amongst a whole pick-and-mix trolley full of her countless failings.

Did she really look such a fright? Was she a freak? Out of place?

Yes, she was definitely out of place, she'd give them that, but when the cruel chatter turned to her scar, and the possibility that Alexander might have caused it, and that was the only reason he tolerated her presence on board his yacht, she'd heard enough. 'Alexander would never do something like this,' she defended him, bursting out of the door.

The women turned to look at her in shock. The heated way in which she had defended him spoke volumes to those who were always alert to the possibility of gossip.

'I was invited on board tonight because of my concern for the waters around Lefkis,' Ellie hurried to explain, 'and only because of that.' But the eyes of her audience had turned blank. She wasn't convincing anyone. More crucially, this was not what they wanted to hear.

So now they thought her not only boring but also bizarre. 'Excuse me,' Ellie said politely, keeping her cool as she eased her way past them.

'Who, or what, are you running from now?'

Ellie gasped and halted right outside the door. The last thing she had been expecting was that Alexander would be waiting for her. 'I'm not running away from anything,' she assured him.

'Really?' he said sardonically.

The time to try the feline smile and half-closed eyes was now, Ellie thought, touching her lips with the tip of her tongue.

The expression of admiration in Alexander's eyes went cold. In its place was a look that iced her heart. Far from enticing him with her sexy look she had apparently caused offence; but how?

Ellie became aware of the deathly silence in the ladies' room. She could imagine all the avid ears pressed up against the door. She knew the women had been speculating wildly on the possibility of a relationship between herself and Alexander. Looked as if now they were about to get proof that he hated her.

She couldn't bear it. She couldn't bear to think of them sharing glances. She couldn't bear to see the expression on Alexander's face—

'What are you playing at, Ellie?'

She flinched at the tone of his voice, but stood her ground. 'I don't know what you mean—'

'Really?' he said in a voice that was even colder if that was possible.

'I don't understand, Alexander. What have I done wrong?'

'You only have to listen to the chatter around the dinner table to know,' he informed her. 'Everyone is commenting on Alexander Kosta's glamorous, if unexpected, new friend; a local girl, a waitress, a fisherman's daughter—'

'And what's wrong with that?' she queried. Alexander had spoken as if each of those was something she should be ashamed of. Should she be ashamed to be considered part of this wonderful island? Should she think the young girl who had let her borrow her waitress's outfit was somehow inferior to her? Should she be ashamed of being a fisherman's daughter, or was it Alexander who should be ashamed for even voicing such thoughts?

'I must say you play the innocent very well,' he rasped as she tipped her chin.

'I have nothing to hide from you, and absolutely nothing to be ashamed of—'

'Nothing?' he cut across her contemptuously. 'Let me look at you.' He studied her from head to toe.

'What's wrong with the way I look?' Ellie demanded. 'I borrowed this dress from a friend—a friend, Alexander,' she said pointedly, wanting now to hurt him as much as he had hurt her. 'And I am a local girl, something that makes me very proud—'

'That's just it, isn't it?' Alexander snapped back. 'You're not a local girl. You're not even Greek—and yet you lose no opportunity to cosy up to the locals and cause me trouble. Why is that, Ellie? Is it just to get close to me?'

'Close to you?' Ellie exclaimed with incredulity. 'I can't think of a single reason why I'd want to do that—'

'Really?' Alexander remarked with a smile that was in no way kind. 'Then you'd better ask all the other women who seek me out and think me an easy touch what I mean. But let me warn you, Ellie Mendoras, that your efforts, just like theirs, are totally wasted on me.'

'My efforts?' Ellie gazed at Alexander in disbelief. 'I think you must be the vainest man I've ever met—' And the most foolish to bracket her with those other women, but because she had vowed to think better of him she tried to hold back from saying that.

'Yes, your efforts,' Alexander railed over her without even listening. 'Just look at you! Look at the way you're dressed. And those looks of yours! You're nothing but a brazen temptress.'

For a moment Ellie was quite pleased with herself, but she quickly got over it. 'You arrogant brute!' she said succinctly, turning on her heels.

He was locked in the past and fighting to find his way back again, Alexander realised, standing rooted to the spot. He literally couldn't stop himself. Seeing Ellie so radically changed in this new and very glamorous outfit had completely thrown him. She had reminded him of his wife; his ex-wife, the bolting bride.

'You're trying too hard,' he called after her, swiping a

tense hand across his brow. 'Don't you know how ridiculous you look?'

She stopped and turned. He could see now that he might as well have slapped her in the face. She was stunned, and as she looked at him he knew that he was wrong, but even so he couldn't help himself; the past had too firm a hold on him.

'You let your hair fly loose, and you pin it up with passion flowers. Did you think I wouldn't notice? Do you take me for a fool?'

'No, Alexander, anything but that. I think you know exactly what you're saying and exactly how much you're hurting me. Congratulations. It must please you to think you can upset me like this.'

He caught up with her and pinned her against the wall. She didn't flinch this time, which made him madder than ever. She was following in his wife's footsteps. First she played the virgin, the fresh, unaffected girl; next the vamp with her pout and her eyes on his money. Did she really believe that was all it took to reel him in?

For one terrible moment Ellie thought Alexander might rip the flowers from her hair, but then she told herself he would never do that, and she just had to wait for him to come back from wherever it was he had journeyed to. She'd seen him mad before, but nothing like this.

'Are you wearing your hair like that just to show off your scar?' he demanded. 'That's what they're saying in there…' He glanced past her towards the dining room.

Not just in there, Ellie was sure, as the silence continued behind the door of the ladies' room. Surely everyone on Alexander's yacht had to be aware of this exchange. Nothing travelled faster than gossip, and reports of this confrontation between them would be all over the island by morning.

'If I reject you, do you think you're going to catch the sympathy vote of one of the other men?'

The other men? The thought had never occurred to her. Ellie touched her cheek, horrified that Alexander could even think that way. 'Are you finished? Can you think of anything nastier to say to me? Or is that it?'

'You look like a tart!' Alexander said, provoked. 'You look like a cheap, stupid tart—'

'And you look like a—' She only broke off because the group of scientists had caught up with them.

'Ah, there she is,' one of them said, smiling as she caught sight of Ellie.

The academics were unaware of what was taking place, Ellie realised. They had to be the only innocents left on board.

The woman confirmed this when she continued blithely on, 'We were just talking about you, my dear, and saying how much we admire your work. We'd love you to join our team—that's if you could find the time. We'd value your local knowledge...'

Ellie nodded numbly. She was still reeling under the on-slaught Alexander had subjected her to and couldn't find her voice. More than that, she didn't trust herself to speak. She had stalled in the dark place Alexander had driven her to. She could see herself through his eyes now—she was a failure as a woman, but, even worse than that, he had seen something in her that the old man must have seen all those years ago. Maybe she was a tart. Maybe she had been responsible for everything that had happened back then. If Alexander believed she was a tease maybe she had led her mother's elderly male friend on. And if that was true then her whole life was built on a lie. She couldn't even call what had happened to her all those years ago rape.

'Thank you,' Ellie managed politely at last. She had to

close her mind to Alexander and concentrate on what really mattered to her if she was going to get through this. 'I'd be delighted to help you,' she told them. And then with more composure than she could have believed herself capable of she turned to Alexander and said calmly, 'Goodnight, Kirie Kosta, and thank you once again for your hospitality…'

'Ellie, come back here.'

Alexander's voice followed Ellie along the corridor, but she refused to listen to him. Her whole concentration was centred on making sure she appeared calm and that her step was measured. She kept her chin up high, telling herself that it no longer mattered what Alexander thought of her. If she could live with herself, and the principles she chose to live by, that was enough.

But it wasn't enough. He had made her feel dirty again; dirty and ashamed.

CHAPTER NINE

HE HAD tossed and turned all night, wondering if he was going mad confusing Ellie with his ex-wife, a woman with a cash register where her heart should have been. He had never doubted Ellie had a heart. Ellie's heart was so big she wanted to change the world and him with it all in the same afternoon. A little ambitious, maybe, especially where he was concerned, Alexander thought drily.

He'd made a mistake; a big one. Calling Ellie a tart, and then seeing her face after he said it, had jolted him into some sort of recognition that this time he might have got it wrong. But she wasn't entirely blameless. He had taken trouble to reassure her by introducing her to scientists who spoke her language. She had repaid him by dressing as his ex-wife might have dressed, with the obvious intention of attracting every man in sight. What was he supposed to think when she had undergone such a radical transformation?

He wanted to believe the best of her, but past experience stood in his way. Looking at the facts, he decided she had picked a cause, put her stake in the ground and gone all out to defy him. There was no question she had invaded his life. Her motives were the only grey area. Now, he could either ignore her and hope she'd go away—which was never going to happen—or he could go see her and straighten things out between them.

He hardened instantly as he thought about the prospect of seeing her again. Maybe facts were no use to him in a situation like this, Alexander conceded wryly. He glanced out of the window at Ellie's little boat, where he could see her moving about. She was tossing buckets of sea water over the deck before scrubbing it down. The way she moved, her suppleness, her strength, her agility…

She had recovered fast after last night. Maybe he had been right thinking her a temptress. Alexander's expression darkened. Ellie Mendoras was no shrinking violet; she was a shrewd and determined woman, who was determined to get her own way. Just because she had more brains than his ex-wife didn't mean he could trust her more; reason dictated he should trust her less. It was time to stop thinking and start doing, Alexander concluded. He wasn't prepared to leave things where they were, Ellie spreading who knew what discontent around his island. She was unpredictable and full of passion. She needed sorting out, and he was in the mood to do it.

Practicalities always saved her and would do so again, Ellie determined. She was desperately hurt and angry after last night, but if she could just concentrate on her tour it might be all right; she might just get over it.

Ellie was meticulous about the routine she had developed. Safety features in particular were never far from her mind. She had already checked the ropes, the dinghy and the life-preservers, and today she had double-checked the radio. She didn't want to make a mistake like that again, or Alexander could see to it that she lost her licence.

Alexander… Alexander… Couldn't she ever get that man

out of her head? After returning from the *Olympus* by taxi last night she had locked herself in the boat and howled until she was completely exhausted. Then she had thrown her pillows round the cabin before reminding herself that she was entirely responsible for her own actions, and for his reaction to them, and that it was up to her to pull herself together.

She had no intention of becoming a victim now, or ever; she'd made that vow to herself some years ago. But she had learned one thing: not trusting men wasn't enough to keep her safe from hurt. How could it be, Ellie thought grimly, if she couldn't trust herself?

After washing, drying and carefully pressing the beautiful dress she had borrowed Ellie put it away until she could return it. She felt sad as she packed it in the carrier bag. After Alexander's ugly accusations the gown she had worn so happily seemed tainted; she had tainted it.

He watched her welcoming people on board the boat from his vantage point at the café table. She had patience, he'd give her that. Half the passengers had never been on a boat before, and had to be asked politely to remove their shoes before walking on the teak deck. She was particularly patient with the older members in the group, and with the mothers who had loaded themselves down with more baggage than they would need on a weekend cruise.

He found it hard to turn away. He found it hard to believe what a good actress she was. But then he already knew that Ellie Mendoras could be anything she wanted to be...Greek, English—whatever suited her on the day. She'd certainly made an amazing turn-around from last night's good-time girl to today's worthy environmentalist.

His wife had been a good actress too, Alexander remembered. And then he remembered the lies she'd told. Lindos was her friend, she'd said; her confidant. The fact that their shared confidences were all destined to take place in the bedroom wasn't supposed to rouse his suspicions. Lindos was an old man who didn't always feel up to getting out of bed, she'd told him.

She'd turned her luminous brown eyes on his face as the lies tripped off her tongue. He'd known. He'd told her to go. And she had gone, without fuss. She had traded him in for a better meal ticket. Or so she'd thought. Of course, he hadn't even begun making his fortune then. The last time he'd seen her she'd been drunk, and was already losing her looks. Lindos beat her, apparently.

And that was the first and last time he'd been taken in by a woman…

Pushing back his chair, Alexander reached inside the back pocket of his jeans to find some change. He had unfinished business to attend to now. No one walked away from him until he said they could, and that included the young woman who was about to leave the harbour on her fishing boat.

The one thing she hadn't noticed was the large yacht moored off shore. How could she have missed it? Ellie wondered, standing stock-still for a moment to stare at the *Olympus*. She always checked she had safe passage out of the harbour before weighing anchor; it was a habit that had served her well in the past, and thank goodness for it now!

Alexander had used a smaller boat to visit the fishermen, but she could only assume that his super-yacht had slipped around the coastline while she was too busy to notice. It made her feel uneasy, as if he was signalling his intention to keep an eye on her.

Well, there was nothing she could do about it, Ellie told herself sensibly. Pulling away from the rail, she prepared to welcome everyone on board and to introduce them round. She didn't need to worry about the sudden appearance of the *Olympus*. Whatever Alexander was here for, it wasn't her! He had made his feelings clear about her last night. He didn't want anything to do with her, which was fine.

Absolutely fine.

She was relieved, in fact.

Tossing her hair out of her eyes, Ellie began her introductory talk.

Having seen everyone comfortably settled in, Ellie looked anxiously at her watch. During the tour she left the boat at various points to collect the specimens she talked about, which meant she needed help. She couldn't be watching the passengers and collecting specimens. To get round this she took one of the local boys with her, but this morning he was late.

Biting her lip, she scanned the harbour. She couldn't afford to leave it much longer or she would miss the tide. All she could hope was that the boy who had been recommended to her for today's tour would turn up soon.

As Ellie turned back to her passengers she was pleased to see that everyone was chatting and getting on well. They looked like a good group. Going to join them, she took up position behind the wheel her father had held. If she closed her eyes she could see him still…strong and tanned, with his weatherbeaten hands gripping this very same wheel. It made her happy to be on his boat, and sad too. The sea she loved and he had loved so well could be so cruel sometimes, and could take the best of men.

Inspired by this, Ellie began telling her first story of the day. Her face lit up as she described exactly how wide her father had spread his hands to introduce her to the ocean. He had told her that it was her heritage, everyone's heritage, and they should take care of it…

And there was no chance she was going to allow Alexander Kosta to destroy that heritage, Ellie vowed silently as everyone murmured agreement with her. She had just moved on to explaining their route for the day when something indefinable changed. It was like an electric current running through the air, a charge that raised all the tiny hairs on the back of her neck.

'I'm not too late, I hope?'

The only thing stopping her from ordering Alexander off the boat immediately was the fact that she couldn't afford to lose her cool in front of all her passengers. But what on earth was he doing here?

For a moment Ellie just stared at Alexander. His expression was pleasantly neutral—she was sure in deference to all the people on board—but there was something in his eyes that warned her not to start anything. She had no intention of doing so and spoiling her passengers' day; so he could stick his challenge! But after all the terrible things he'd said to her last night, how dare he walk onto her boat as if he owned it? 'What do you want here, Alexander?'

'That's not quite the welcome I had expected,' he admitted to the amusement of the small crowd. Ellie could see that no one could quite believe who had walked on board. Everyone there knew Alexander Kosta; who didn't know the man who had added an island to his weekly shopping list?

Unlike Ellie, Alexander appeared to be completely relaxed. He was comfortably slouched on one hip with his hand resting on the rope by his side, as if his sole purpose in life was to flaunt his masculinity. And just to complete the picture he had chosen to wear the uniform of a local fisherman, which comprised little more than a sun-faded vest and cut-off jeans. He looked...

Ellie refused categorically to think about how Alexander looked. A muscle was working in his jaw as he gazed at her and he held her gaze just long enough to let her know he wasn't going anywhere. Once he had delivered that message he turned away and went, confident of his warm reception, to greet her passengers.

So the frantic mind messages clearly hadn't worked, Ellie raged inwardly. Alexander was as comfortable here as on his yacht. He had simply slipped into his casual, friendly, relaxed persona with absolutely no trouble at all. The same confidence and natural ease she had seen at work on the podium when he gave his speech about the changes to the island made everyone instantly comfortable, effectively removing the gulf between Alexander's massively privileged status and their more humdrum lives. Her passengers loved him. Pity the same couldn't be said for her. All in all his lethal charm had taken around ten seconds to work its magic, Ellie fumed, wishing she could think of a way to throw him off.

Short of a miracle, she was stuck with him, she realised, heart racing as she watched him shaking hands and spending time with each member of her group. She could see how impressed they were. Alexander Kosta was definitely an 'A' list celebrity, and none of her group had been expecting to meet him today. Plus he was hot, of course, a fact that she and every other woman on board had instantly registered.

First off there was the glow of wealth you couldn't fake, and then there was the aura of success he carried with him. Everyone hoped a little of it would rub off on them. The end result was that Alexander was undeniably a power source; a people magnet. He could hold the interest of her group just as long as he wanted to. And relegate her to the sidelines until it suited him.

'Have you finished working my audience?' Ellie hissed at him the moment Alexander returned to her side.

'Not nearly,' he said with a wicked smile.

'So, why are you here, Alexander? Have you come along just to insult me some more?'

'Depends—'

'On what?' Ellie cut across him angrily.

'On how well you behave yourself…'

She hoped he was joking and moved away. The way they were speaking, in an unnatural whisper, meant they had to stand way too close. Gritting her teeth, Ellie glanced at the shore. 'Well, now you've made your royal progress you can get off my boat.'

'That's not very gracious of you, Ellie.'

'Get off or swim. I'm leaving harbour now—'

'I'm not going anywhere.'

She snapped around to spear a look at him. The way Alexander had his naked feet planted firmly on her deck suggested she might have to call the police if she wanted him removed. *Alexander's police…they worked for him now.* 'This is piracy.'

The brow quirked, the lips tugged and still he didn't move. 'And all these good people will be your witnesses in court against me, I presume?'

No wonder Alexander always looked so confident. He knew he had her tied up in knots every which way she turned. And since he owned everything else on the island she could only presume he had the judges in his pocket too. She was powerless against him, Ellie realised, sucking in an angry breath. She turned her back on her little group in the hopes they would remain unaware of the drama being played out just yards away from them. 'You are despicable—'

'I've been called worse things,' Alexander told her calmly.

Short of an attitude that left him in no doubt as to how she felt about him, she was stuck with him, and he knew it.

'Shouldn't we be leaving harbour now?' he said, all innocence.

'There is no *we*, Alexander.' But he was right. The tide was turning. She could detect the rhythm of the water changing under the deck beneath her naked feet. Her father had taught her how to feel the different currents running beneath the boat, and in this new shallow harbour she had to be aware, or they could become grounded on a sandbank. How Mr Arrogant and Smug would love that!

She didn't dare to think about her father now, Ellie realised, turning away from Alexander. She didn't dare allow Alexander to see a single feeling on her face that wasn't cold detestation. He might have invaded her private space—hell, her life too—but he was so sure he had bettered her, and no way was she going to give him the satisfaction of seeing her upset. As of now she had one simple decision to make. She could cancel the tour, or leave harbour immediately.

As she turned back to glare at him she saw he was just wiping his tanned brow on a powerful forearm. He stilled, watching her watching him.

She couldn't remain immune to Alexander however hard she tried, Ellie concluded with frustration. His usually well-groomed hair was wind-ruffled, and all the better for it, in her opinion; a hank of it was falling over his eyes. She could almost believe the inky-black waves had softened his features.

They clung to the back of his neck, and to his cheekbones. And strange things were happening to her insides as she watched that thick black hair blowing around his face...

Time to go, Ellie told herself grimly; she'd done enough ego-massaging for one day just by staring at him. She checked down the quay one last time, silently begging the boy she had been expecting to appear. No such luck.

'Looks like you've got no alternative but to take me on as crew...'

'Are you offering your assistance?' Grinding her jaw with frustration, Ellie rounded on Alexander.

'Do you need it?'

This time he didn't even try to hold back his grin.

'OK, I'll give you a trial,' she agreed grudgingly.

Alexander gave her a mock-bow, and then, turning around he got started, untying ropes and generally preparing for casting off. If he was here to find fault she'd sling him overboard, Ellie decided grimly, not quite sure how she would manage it, only that she would.

'Is this your way of silencing me? Revoking my licence to trade? What?' she demanded under her breath as they worked together side by side.

'Why, Ellie, you're so suspicious,' Alexander said, faking disappointment in her. 'Don't you trust me?'

'Not one bit.' She stared at him coldly, trying not to see him as a man. She failed. By any standards Alexander was a luscious masculine specimen, so deeply tanned and hard-muscled he looked like the marauding pirate she already believed him to be. 'Trust has to be earned, Alexander.'

He seemed amused by this and raised a brow. 'Promise to do better, boss...'

'Start by getting that anchor up,' Ellie snapped back,

refusing to be won over. 'There's too much work to do to stand here talking to you.'

'Aye aye, Captain...'

She narrowed her eyes, trying to ignore the smooth way Alexander swung on a rope as he passed by.

'Does the fact that you've taken me on mean you're throwing in the towel already?' he murmured in passing.

'And make it easy for you?' His face was far too close, far, *far* too close. 'Forget it, Alexander.' Assuming a disdainful expression, Ellie willed her pulse to calm down, but she felt sure Alexander must see it banging in her neck. Didn't she know by now he missed nothing?

'Sorry,' he murmured penitently.

He was no such thing.

Alexander brushed past her from time to time as he went about his allocated tasks. Each time she gasped. Each time she tried to hide the fact. And each time she failed. The bare fact was he felt so good. He felt solid and safe.

Unfortunately, it was inevitable that they would touch on a boat. This was what Ellie told herself as they worked close and fast together. That was just the way it was, and she had to get over it.

After a while instead of dreading his touch, she found herself wondering when the next one would come along. And when she could she watched him covertly, enjoying the sight of him working, stripped to the waist and using that strong, tanned body of his to the full. As entertainment went, it wasn't half bad.

After last night she had told herself she never wanted to see him again, but now she wasn't quite so sure. Just watching Alexander catch a mooring line was educational...and OK, arousing.

As the old fishing smack slowly cruised out of the harbour

Ellie couldn't help noticing how Alexander had slipped into an easy routine as crew, as if he had been born to it.

Which, of course, he had, Ellie remembered. The great Alexander Kosta had been born in simple circumstances on a neighbouring island, and had more claim to being an islander than she did. What a pity he'd lost touch with the people he professed to care about. Of course, this could always be an attempt to get back to those roots... Or maybe it was simply an opportunity to find an excuse to boot her off the island. Either way, she had to admit he had completed the tasks she'd set him in a fraction of the time anyone else might have taken.

Ellie cut her daydreams short abruptly when Alexander came loping with his easy stride towards her across the deck. 'Any more orders for me, Captain?' he said with irony, staring into her eyes in a way that was downright insubordinate.

'Yes, answer me this truthfully. Why are you here, Alexander?'

'Unfinished business...'

'Unfinished,' Ellie said with disbelief. 'I can't believe you left a thing unsaid last night, unless you've remembered some insults you forgot to fling at me.' She held his gaze in spite of the way that made her feel. But then she was forced to break off. Her passengers had relaxed and were starting to chat to her.

Ellie slipped into another groove right away. How could she not agree how lucky they were to be out on the sea today? The water was so smooth, and the sunshine felt wonderful on her skin. But even when she threw her head back and revelled in the cooling breeze like everyone else she was still distracted by Alexander. He had started unfurling the sails high above their heads, and was walking across the yard arm in bare feet... He'd rolled up his jeans, revealing powerful,

powerful muscles on his calves. She had to quickly look away again and try to concentrate. Too late. She'd already downloaded the type of visual information into her memory banks that stuck around.

Alexander had picked his battleground well, Ellie reflected, and after last night she had to remain suspicious of his motives. No way was she going to stand around and take his insults here. This was her boat; her world. She kept her powder dry until he joined her at the wheel. 'Just tell me what you want, Alexander, and then we can leave each other alone for the rest of the trip...'

'I can't do that,' he said flatly, smiling at her passengers while doing his best to disconcert Ellie.

'And why's that?'

'Because I want to get to know you; because it's my business to know everything that goes on within my sphere of influence—'

'Your sphere of influence?' Ellie burst out, remembering too late she had to curb her inclination to let him have it with both barrels. 'I think you'd better read up on maritime law, Alexander. This is my boat, not your island; you have no jurisdiction here.'

'Except when you return to port,' he murmured very close to her ear.

Her ear tingled. Everything tingled. She was acutely conscious of him standing close by; their arms were almost touching. She didn't move; why should she? This was her boat...

'My port,' Alexander emphasised softly, again raising all the tiny hairs on the back of her neck.

'Don't threaten me,' Ellie warned, but when she turned to look at him her heart started to thunder. Alexander's eyes were just so incredible; incredibly cruel, merciless and hard.

She looked away again, tilting her chin at an unmistakable angle of defiance.

But soon Ellie's thoughts began to wander. She'd never kissed a man properly. That old man back in England had seen to that. How could she when she associated contact with a man with violence? Until Alexander kissed her she'd never been remotely tempted.

It took all she'd got for Ellie to jerk back to reality. But she soon recovered when she realised that Alexander was talking to her passengers again...

'We look set fair for a pleasant cruise,' he was saying to them. Or was he talking to her? Ellie wondered as he glanced at her. *A pleasant cruise?* Did he think she was going to chat to him, or attempt to make a friend of him after last night?

When she was quite sure no one was listening she challenged him. 'I'm surprised you want to spend your precious free time with a tart...'

'This is all part of getting to know my world—'

'Lucky for me I'm not part of your world.'

'I thought you lived on Lefkis?'

'Alexander, if you don't mind, I've got a boat to sail.' Angling herself away from him so she would no longer have to look into those complex and disturbing eyes, Ellie concentrated on sailing.

'I'm here to help you, Ellie,' Alexander pointed out, 'and we've a long day ahead of us—'

'Then get used to being ignored,' she told him tartly. 'I know why you're here—'

'Really? Perhaps you would care to enlighten me.'

'You're here to spy... You're here to judge—'

'And you always judge me too harshly.'

'Oh, do I really?' Ellie said, pretending surprise. 'I wonder why that is?' Her brows rose sharply as she turned to stare at him. 'Perhaps you could tell me what happened to the boy who was supposed to be working with me on board today?'

'I gave him the day off. I trust I'm a suitable replacement?'

'You're a replacement,' Ellie conceded, 'but in future leave the choice of my staff to me—'

'Staff?'

At last! She'd scored a point! She felt like cheering. But instead she pinned a serious expression on her face before turning to look at him. 'No one asked you to put yourself in this position, Alexander. You did that all by yourself. And now,' she said before he had chance to answer her, 'it's time for you to do the rounds and see if anyone would like a drink.'

He looked at her; she held his gaze. Levelly. It was easy to see that Alexander Kosta hadn't taken instructions in quite some time.

They had reached one of Ellie's all-time favourite places, and in good time thanks to the strong wind and good weather. It was another rocky outcrop small enough for the weakest swimmers to paddle round in safety. From past experience Ellie knew that everyone would go home with a sense of achievement if they could swim all the way round the tiny island.

Ellie couldn't help feeling a flutter of resentment as she watched Alexander sorting out the group's fins and snorkels. He was good, but that was her job. In fairness, he had a way with people, but she wasn't going down the road of believing he was capable of change just because of that.

However, the day was proving to be an eye-opener where Alexander was concerned. Ellie hadn't considered the possibility that he might love the ocean as much as she did. She was just reflecting on it when Alexander turned to look at her.

It was as if he knew what she was thinking. That was also her cue to look away. But she didn't manage it before her heart was pounding.

It was a relief to be able to immerse herself in practical activities, Ellie reflected as she collected up all the surplus tackle and stowed it away. But now there was another problem looming: she had to strip off. She was happy to do that when she was surrounded by families and children, but today was different, because today Alexander was on the boat.

Ellie started to get ready with everyone else, but she was already feeling hugely self-conscious and she hadn't taken her shorts off yet. All she had to do was strip down to her swimming costume. And there was nothing remotely provocative about it. Her costume was a proper costume for proper swimming, though after his comments last night Alexander probably expected her to wear something skimpy with tassels.

Too bad she had to disappoint him…not.

As soon as everyone was ready Ellie made her final checks to be sure the boat was secure. Alexander seemed to have made a point of keeping out of her way since they'd dropped anchor. She could hear him now, making everyone feel at ease. She felt like pulling faces at him. It seemed that laughter was the new language on board, and Alexander had appointed himself the teacher.

It was a pity he couldn't be civil to her, Ellie thought as she secured a towel round her chest. She flashed a glance in his direction. Alexander hadn't stripped off as yet. He was occupied at present, helping an elderly lady down the ladder at the side of the boat and into the sea. His whole concentration was fixed on that.

Alexander Kosta playing Sir Lancelot? He had blindsided

her. Who would have thought Alexander had a caring bone in his body?

Once the old lady was safely launched Ellie joined the queue to disembark. First problem: she had to go past Alexander before she could enter the water. She tried relaxing, but the closer it came to her turn the more she wanted to avoid him and dive in.

Unfortunately, she couldn't do that; she had the container for the specimens slung across her shoulder. 'Excuse me, please…'

'I'll help you down,' he said, turning to her when the last passenger was safely in the water.

'I'd rather you moved aside…'

'I'm sure you would,' he said without moving.

Ellie stared at Alexander's outstretched hand. Did she want to take it?

'Come on,' he said, 'this isn't about you and me, this is about safety precautions. You know you can't keep your passengers down there in the ocean on their own. You have to join them, Ellie…'

Alexander was right. Swallowing her pride she took his hand. 'Thank you,' she said politely without meeting his gaze.

As she climbed down the ladder Ellie knew Alexander was above her, and he didn't move until he was sure she was safe in the sea.

CHAPTER TEN

She was a strong swimmer, and, even though she was hampered by a container, it didn't take Ellie long to reach her charges. She soon had everyone clustered around the rocks watching closely as she uncovered a vast array of wildlife they hadn't even spotted.

'It's just familiarity,' she said, brushing off her talent for locating the tiny creatures she loved. She went on answering the barrage of questions until she realised she'd lost her audience.

Turning in the direction everyone else was looking, Ellie saw why she had lost her audience. Alexander was standing on the swaying rail at the side of the boat, preparing to dive in. He looked amazing. Like a thunderbolt it struck her how it felt to hold his hand. He *was* amazing. She hadn't felt like this *ever* before. Which meant it was high time she turned away to concentrate on something safer.

What had she been expecting? That he kept his jeans and vest on to swim? Ellie tried not to think what she'd seen. She tried not to look. She would not look. *She would not...* She looked.

And now her heart was beating so fast she couldn't hear herself think. Alexander's body was immense. And in all the right places. Suspecting that it might be was one thing, but seeing that it was was something else. She had to turn right round and look again... *She simply had to!*

Alexander's muscles pulsed and flexed as he plunged towards the sea. He was sculpted in bronze and outlined in sunlight. His dive was perfect, and so was he. His control was something else. He entered the water with barely a splash.

Ellie had to turn her face to the rock to compose herself. So he could dive well? What was that? Thousands of people could dive well. But she hadn't been admiring just his technique, Ellie admitted to herself, giving a little shriek when Alexander surfaced right next to her. Had he swum the whole way underwater? He was good. Not that she was going to let him see she was impressed, of course. 'You've left the boat unattended.'

'Everything's secure. I made sure the anchor was safely bedded in.'

'You dived down to the seabed...' *As well?*

'Of course... How else would I know that?'

She'd lost this one, Ellie realised as the children began to laugh.

'The captain wasn't available for me to ask for instructions at the time,' Alexander explained, winking at his audience. 'But I am in a position to assure you that everything's safe, and no pirates have been sighted—'

'I wouldn't be too sure about that,' Ellie said pointedly, quirking one brow.

'There's not a chance we'll be attacked,' Alexander told her to a chorus of complaint.

As he shook the hair out of his eyes Ellie realised how close their naked limbs were in the water. 'How can you be so sure?' she said to entertain the children.

'Simple. I have the coast patrolled.'

Of course he did. Her expression hardened. How could she forget that this was his coast, his patrol, his island? 'Well, I decide what's safe on my boat, and I'm ordering you back on board, sailor.'

'And what will you do to me if I won't go?'

There were a number of things that sprang to mind. Ellie knew she should turn away and get on with her search for interesting specimens, but…

But her senses were screaming, and her mind was fully occupied by weighing up the expression in Alexander's eyes. The one thing she could be sure about was that it was playing havoc with her pulse. Why didn't he say something? Do something? Did he have to keep staring at her like that?

Determinedly, Ellie composed her features into her most teacherly mask, and got on with her job. It took a lot of care to remove a conveniently placed sea anemone from its rocky nest.

'I like the way you handle them…'

'Haven't you gone yet?' she murmured to him under her breath. She would not look at him. There were too many people around, and Alexander's voice was far too close to her ear. Their naked legs were almost touching, making it so hard for her to concentrate.

And now the children were laughing again thanks to Alexander pulling faces behind her back. He had everyone on his side. OK, so maybe she was in danger of taking herself too seriously today, but Alexander wasn't helping. 'These sea anemones are meat-eaters,' Ellie explained, determined to carry on with her informative talk in spite of him. 'And, as Alexander pointed out, you have to handle them with the greatest care. I'm going to put this one into our container so that we can talk about it in more depth when we get back on the boat…'

She had to try very hard not to notice Alexander slicking his thick black hair from his face as he watched her transferring the small, flower-like creature to the container slung over her shoulder. 'Would you hold that for me, Alexander?' She could get used to this, Ellie thought wryly. Ordering him about was beginning to grow on her. But she wasn't going to wait to see his reaction. Securing her mask, she sank gratefully beneath the water where he couldn't see her flushed cheeks and went in search of more sea life.

'Shall I find you something?' Alexander suggested when she surfaced again.

'Yes, why don't you?' And give me a breather from that penetrating stare, Ellie thought, taking off her mask to shake her own hair back.

'The baby octopus was a lucky find,' Alexander explained to her group a little later.

He'd done well. He was amazing, Ellie conceded. Her group was fascinated by everything Alexander had brought up from the deeper water. If she didn't hate him quite so much she would have had to say they made a great team.

'Why don't we all go back on board now so Ellie can tell you about the creatures we have collected?' Alexander suggested.

'You're giving orders now?' Ellie murmured as everyone obediently started back.

'If you'll excuse me, Ellie,' Alexander said with a definite glint in his eyes, 'I don't have time to chat now. I have people to help back on board...'

She watched him swim away, wishing she could come up with a reasonable excuse to keel-haul him, or make him walk the plank. Did men come any more infuriating than this one? If they did it was high time she joined a nunnery.

Ellie watched Alexander eat up the distance between the rocks and the boat in a matter of seconds with his easy freestyle stroke. She couldn't deny he was working hard to make this trip a success. But then she reminded herself that

Alexander Kosta had perfected the technique of getting what he wanted out of life. The only question now was, what was he after this time?

Alexander stayed in the sea until the last of Ellie's passengers was safely back on board, and then he listened attentively to her talk without interrupting her once. He even helped her to serve the lunch and drinks, and did all that without any of his previous mocking comments. In spite of how she'd felt about him earlier Ellie found herself mellowing; fractionally.

He came down into the galley to help her clear up after lunch while everyone else was relaxing on deck.

'You don't need to—'

'It was very quiet down here. I thought I'd better see if you were OK…'

'You're doing too much thinking, Alexander. I'm just fine.'

'That's good to hear, Ellie, but it looks to me like you could do with a hand. There's a lot to clear up before we start back.'

Her glance slid away from his. 'I'm relaxed; I can do it. I'll take my time.'

'And I'll help you. Flag of truce?' Alexander suggested, flourishing a cloth.

'You're going to help me dry the dishes? I wish I had a camera to record the moment—'

He smiled, and it had a devastating effect on her. 'Lucky for me, then, that you don't…'

And now they were working side by side again. Close; very close. 'It's been a good day, don't you think?' Ellie commented in an attempt to distract herself.

'You're good.'

'Compliments from you, Alexander? Surely not…'

'I give compliments where they're due…'

Was she supposed to curtsey at this point? Ellie wondered. 'Why, thank you, sir,' she managed meekly.

'I like that,' Alexander approved. 'We must have more humility on the part of women on the island now I own it. Perhaps I could pass a law...'

'And perhaps I could do something quite drastic if you do,' Ellie warned him. *Was she flirting with him?* Her face flamed red at the thought.

Trying not to make it too obvious that she was putting some much needed space between them, she moved away. But it wasn't all that easy to find space in a tiny galley kitchen.

He was only here because he didn't like loose ends. He'd told her that already. How many times did he have to tell himself the same thing?

He had been so angry with her last night; filled with suspicion. He had examined the faces of all the men on board to see if any of them were looking at her. He knew now that he had been locked in the past, thinking about another woman. His bride had been quite different from Ellie—shallow water, where she was deep.

But there was another reason he was here. She was advertising her tours on the internet, and he had to be sure that they were safe and that he was happy for the reputation of the island to be hanging on them. From what he'd seen Ellie was certainly up to the task. In fact her talks were inspirational; she was inspirational. Her enthusiasm for the natural world was infectious. The only problem he had detected so far was that she really didn't know how good she was.

And she couldn't possibly know how much he wanted her. Easing his shoulders in the cramped space, he wanted to kiss her again—and much more. He could feel her warmth beside him like a homing beacon. Even her volatile temperament excited him; Ellie was unpredictable, just like the ocean she loved. The thought of being in bed with her and turning all that heated passion in his direction was—

Something he mustn't think about now.

The muted sound of happy voices up on deck soothed Ellie to the point where she managed to forget the threat Alexander posed. She hadn't realised she had drawn so congenially close to him until he looked down at her and she felt his fresh, warm breath on her face.

'Something troubling you?' he said when she swiftly moved away.

Only her own recklessness. 'Nothing…' She shook her head to underscore the point. But even as she spoke the single word Alexander lifted his hand and brushed her lips very lightly with one finger.

'I think you're hiding something from me,' Alexander murmured.

She needed air. Now! Alexander's touch…in fact, the fact that he had touched her at all was something she needed space to think about.

Stacking plates and getting on with her practical tasks was the best therapy, Ellie decided. She couldn't rush up on deck leaving Alexander to clear up alone…but his touch on her lips wouldn't disappear; she could still feel it.

As she went to move past him to open another cupboard, instead of getting out of her way Alexander stayed exactly where he was. She was already committed to moving into the tiny space, and now she was trapped and pressed up hard against him.

As her hands rose to push him away something happened. It happened the moment she made contact with Alexander's hard, unyielding chest. First all her strength drained out of her, and then, instead of pushing him away her fingers tangled in his vest and she clung on tight.

'So you do trust me now?' Alexander was smiling down at her.

Why didn't she just pull away? What was happening to her? The tension between them was overwhelming. 'I'd better get back up on deck and make sure everyone has everything they need,' she said, struggling for composure. That was a lot better; she was seeing sense at last...

Or not.

She could only feel disappointed when Alexander moved away, holding up his hands to show he had no intention of touching her. When would she get it through her head that Alexander wasn't interested in her that way?

To add insult to injury he took the steps of the companion-way two at a time until he had disappeared into the sunlight. He didn't look back at her once, and soon she heard him laughing with the passengers. She followed shortly afterwards, having renewed her pledge to make today special for them.

Everyone grew quiet and drowsy as they sailed back to port. Ellie didn't feel like speaking either until the boat passed the spot where Alexander's men had strung chains across the channel.

'It was a necessary precaution,' he said, seeing her looking.

People would expect more of an explanation than that, Ellie thought.

'I've had scientists check the route out in advance,' he said, she guessed to reassure her. 'The impact on the ocean will be minimal, I assure you, but I do understand your concerns—'

'Are Ellie's concerns valid?' someone asked him.

Ellie tensed. She didn't want to get into a full-blown argument while she had passengers on board, and with the way things stood between her and Alexander there was every chance of that happening. 'We're working through them together,' she said, indulging in a necessary white lie. 'As you know, Alexander is a reasonable man...' She crossed her fingers. 'Isn't that right, Alexander?' She flashed him a big smile.

'That's why I'm here today,' he agreed, picking up her cue. 'I want to reassure Ellie that there will only be change for the better on Lefkis.'

There was a flash in his eyes that no one else saw. If that wasn't a warning shot across her bows, she didn't know what was. But she couldn't think about that now; it was enough that everyone was happy with the answer Alexander had given them, and was settling down again.

While Alexander took his turn at the wheel Ellie spent her time with those people who were interested in learning more about the local sea life. There was also a lot of interest in the forthcoming power-boat race, she noted, as well as much talk of future holidays being planned to coincide with them if there were more.

Maybe compromise was the answer, Ellie conceded as she went to take over at the wheel. It was important for her to have control now because they were approaching a stretch of water she could never pass by without remembering that it was here that her father had lost his life.

As always she cut the engines and cruised past slowly; reverently. No one but her knew that the patch of deceptively smooth water was like a shrine to her.

In spite of the various undercurrents throughout, Ellie deemed the day a success. She was still passing out contact numbers for future tours when she noticed Alexander lowering a bucket into the sea in readiness to sluice down the decks. He had no intention of leaving with the others when they docked; far from it. He was enjoying himself, she realised. As they tied up he was throwing himself into the work, and calling out to the fishermen alongside as if he was one of them…

Dropping the mantle of Greek tycoon had been so swift and complete Ellie stood transfixed where she was for a moment. It was hard to believe Alexander could turn into this relaxed—and yes, almost pleasant being. His face had eased into that of a man at peace with his world, and with himself.

And how long did she think that was going to last? Ellie asked herself sensibly.

'Are you going to stand there all day doing nothing?'

She realised Alexander was leaning on his brush, staring at her.

'I've got it,' she said, trying to wrest the broom from him. 'You can go home now.'

'I'm staying until we've finished—'

'Like I said, Alexander, there is no *we*… And you have finished.'

Predictably, he ignored her. 'I'll stow everything away for you—'

'No need…' Ellie made a sound of frustration as Alexander's head disappeared beneath the hatchway. But then he bobbed up again—just half of him—the impressive torso and mocking face. 'Why don't you join me for a cold beer when you're finished?'

Because I'm not insane? 'Because it's stuffy down there, and I prefer to stay up here on deck—'

'I meant come for a drink with me on the quayside when we're finished…' Leaning his forearms on the deck, Alexander stared at her in a way Ellie guessed every woman on earth would find disarming.

But not her.

'Do I take your silence for a yes? That's good,' Alexander remarked before she had chance to reply. 'We'll have supper on shore. I know a great place…fresh fish, music, dancing…'

Her mind had blanked. Why was she agreeing to this? Silence was as good as agreement in this instance. And then to make matters worse she realised that several of the fishermen had stopped working to listen to this exchange. No doubt they were as riveted as she was: was *the* Alexander Kosta asking local girl Ellie Mendoras out on a date?

'You must be hungry,' Alexander reasoned, filling in the silence. 'I know I am. And isn't that what we both need?'

'What do we need?' Ellie said, instantly suspicious.

'Food,' he said, as if that were obvious. 'Good food, soft lights, sweet music and a big bowl of Greek salad with feta cheese, olives…'

The fishermen winked at her.

Right on cue, her stomach growled. 'OK, I'd like that,' she reluctantly agreed.

'What's that for?' Ellie said, gazing at the bowl of fresh parsley the smiling restaurateur had just placed in front of them.

'Chew it,' Alexander instructed.

'Er, why?'

'Because parsley is the best thing to chew after eating onions…' Alexander smiled his wicked smile at her, revealing perfect white and even teeth.

'Are you suggesting my breath smells of onions?' Ellie demanded with affront, knowing it must.

'I'm not planning to get close enough to find out,' Alexander told her disappointingly, 'but our host clearly thinks I might want to—'

'More fool him,' Ellie huffed, as if the idea of Alexander kissing her hadn't occurred to her constantly throughout the meal. His hair was tousled, and his eyes were a vivid green. And after a day out on the water his face was even more tanned, if that was possible. They were surrounded by seamen, all in a similar state of contented disarray... But none of them could hold a candle to Alexander, Ellie decided. Which of course was immaterial, since she wasn't interested. She had to quickly refocus when she realised that Alexander had caught her staring at him. To do something—anything—to distract him she grabbed a handful of parsley and crammed it in her mouth. 'It tastes disgusting,' she said between chomping.

'I'll have to take your word for that.'

'Aren't you going to eat any?'

'Like I said. I'm not planning any close encounters of the amatory kind, so it's hardly relevant...'

Oh, really... Well, that was nice!

'Well, thank you.' She pushed up from the table. She was getting just a little bit fed up with Alexander loading the gun so she could shoot herself in the foot. 'I'm just going to wash my hands...' To cool down. And regroup. And gather her scrambled wits together.

As always Alexander appeared to be the perfect gentleman, standing and holding her chair as she left the table. But as she walked across the room Ellie could feel his burning gaze scorching into her back every step of the way.

CHAPTER ELEVEN

'WOULD you like to dance, Ellie?'

The music started up and people had begun to dance. He'd made her feel on edge as she sat up close and personal with him in the restaurant—did she have the courage to dance with him? He invoked furious passion within her. Was she ready for some more? She couldn't hide from how he made her feel. She couldn't pretend he didn't steal her breath away…

'I'd love to…'

It was that easy. Alexander crooked his little finger and she melted into a puddle of desire at his feet. Yet she knew to be wary of him…didn't she?

She glanced at his outstretched hand and then past him towards the dance floor. A traditional bouzouki band was playing and everyone was dancing together in one big circle. It was harmless fun. For goodness' sake, little boys were dancing with their grandmothers, and from a corner of the room Kiria Theodopulos was nodding encouragement.

She was safe. It was safe. Alexander was safe. If she danced with him it represented a big step forward for her. The look in Alexander's clear green gaze was offering her nothing more than a dance. While she was still thinking about it he caught hold of her hand and led her into the ever-widening circle of dancers.

She hadn't been dancing for such a long time, Ellie realised as Alexander smiled and drew her closer to his side, but as the music slowed to a sexy rumba rhythm she tensed and tried to move away from him.

'Had enough?' he said.

Couples all around them were dancing cheek to cheek, bodies moving sinuously in time to the beat. In a way she never could, Ellie realised. She would only make a fool of herself. One, she had no rhythm, and two, she had no confidence to press up close to Alexander. Yet, considering he was so much bigger than she was, they fitted together perfectly... But there was always something else, something clouding her judgement and stopping her relaxing.

'Something wrong?'

'No, nothing,' Ellie said distractedly as she wove her way across the crowded dance floor. Nothing? She could already feel the stealthy tread of fear creeping down her spine. She couldn't trust herself with Alexander.

He stared her in the eyes as he settled her in her seat. 'Nothing?' he repeated with disbelief. 'So *nothing* makes you tense up like this? *Nothing* makes you shy away from me?' He shook his head. 'There's more, and you're not telling me—'

'There's nothing more,' she said, breaking away from him.

Stumbling over people's feet, she kept going. People looked at her, but this wasn't the time to stop and explain that Alexander's physicality frightened her. The intensity of the situation and her own feelings frightened her. That, and the fact that the contemptuous laugh of the old man who had attacked her was ringing in her head.

When she got outside Ellie realised Alexander was right behind her.

'Don't you think it's time you told me what this is about?'

She shook him off when he tried to take hold of her arm. 'Go back to your friends!' She gestured jerkily in the direction of the café.

'No, Ellie, I want to be with you—'

At that moment a man brushed by them. He was smoking a big cigar. Ellie lost it completely. Blood started pounding through her veins. She couldn't hear Alexander. He was speaking, but she couldn't hear him...

'Come back here, Ellie—'

She wasn't stopping for anything. She ran into the night, seeking darkness, seeking shadows. But Alexander caught up with her. He slowed and approached carefully, as if fearing she might bolt again.

Pressed up against cold stone in a corner of the harbour wall, Ellie slowly sank to the ground. Then, drawing up her knees, she wrapped her arms around them and buried her face in them to shut him out.

'Ellie...'

Alexander hunkered down beside her.

'I'm so sorry...' She kept her face hidden. 'I know how badly I've behaved, and I apologise.' *Now go away. I can't bear you to see me like this. I can't bear anyone to see me like this and feel pity for me...* Gradually, she became aware that Alexander hadn't moved or touched her. He hadn't spoken. He was just there, breathing easily at her side; there if she needed him. She turned her face slightly to look at him. 'Sorry,' she whispered, 'don't know what came over me.'

Neither did he, but he was going to find out—whatever it took, and however long it took him. He didn't try to help her when she got up. She needed space; he knew that. He'd encountered people who'd suffered trauma before, and he knew how clever they could be at hiding behind a mask. He also knew what could happen when that mask came down. She would need someone to be there for her then. He would be there for her.

The realisation hit him like a thunderbolt. When was the last time he'd wanted to reach out to anyone?

'It's been a long day…'

He refocused and looked at her.

'I'm ready to turn in,' she added. 'Hope you don't mind?'

'I'll walk you to the boat,' he said, careful to keep his distance in speech and deed.

They walked side by side. He was glad when her step became more confident. He wasn't going to push her; in any direction. She was strong, but she was vulnerable. She had set up business in a foreign land and renovated an old boat single-handedly in order to do so, but there was a lot more than that to Ellie Mendoras.

'Alexander, thank you,' she said formally when they reached the gangway of her boat. 'I'm sorry I broke down like that. I was thinking about my father—'

True or not, he would go along with it for now. 'Ellie, I'm so sorry—'

'I know you are.'

She cut him off. She didn't want any meaningless platitudes. She was right; he'd never known the man. But what he'd just witnessed had been terror, not sorrow. He went fishing for answers. 'Just so long as you're not frightened of me—'

'Of course I'm frightened of you, Alexander,' she said, faintly teasing him. 'Shouldn't every sensible woman quake when she's spoken to by the great Alexander Kosta?'

'So, you're sensible now?'

Their eyes held. The brief flash of amusement in Ellie's was enough for him.

Enough for what? How could he say that when what he wanted to do now was sweep her into his arms and make love to her? 'You should be quaking,' he insisted, holding her gaze.

'Really?' she said, drawing her brows together as she thought about it. 'There must be something wrong with me.'

Nothing that I can see.

'Oh, and that reminds me,' she said, bringing him back down to earth again. 'I haven't paid you for your work today.'

'Let's call it quits, shall we?'

'Well, at least let me pay for the meal…'

'It will keep, Ellie. Get a good night's rest.' He turned to go.

She called him back.

'What?'

A moment passed, and then another one. The night was full of possibilities…

'Nothing,' she said, breaking the mood. 'Just…' She shrugged. 'Thank you.'

'My pleasure, Ellie…' He gave her a mock-bow. The urge to kiss her was stronger than ever; it was just a shame he'd seen the pain hiding behind the smile she'd got pinned to her face.

Ellie groaned. She had slept heavily. The second she opened her eyes the events of the night came flooding back. Including horrible, stomach-wrenching 'making a fool of herself' moments. She'd done everything she'd vowed never to do. She'd let her feelings out and shared them around. It couldn't happen again. Not with Alexander. What had she been thinking?

Clutching her head, Ellie scrambled free of the covers. Kneeling up in front of the porthole, she stared out, looking for the *Olympus*. Of course, it wasn't there. Everything had changed. She wasn't thinking straight. Would she ever think straight when it came to Alexander?

She went up on deck with an old crocheted blanket round her shoulders. There was nothing but empty ocean as far as she could see.

She had to get ready for that morning's cruise. She had to shut out a man so far out of her league he shouldn't even raise a blip on her radar.

The same man her heart was aching for as if it was never going to recover, Ellie thought, shading her eyes as she stared out across the sea. She had been working flat out to get the boat ready, and it hadn't helped at all. She could usually lose herself in work, but not today. The ocean had never looked so empty to her before. Fortunately, just before the lump had time to form in her throat she caught sight of the first of her passengers coming down the quay.

Ellie went to greet them with the same enthusiasm she always showed. The more people who started to love the ocean as much as she did the better.

She steered a course to her favourite little island. The day went well and she was enjoying the slow cruise back when she saw something that made her shout a warning. Moving fast, she brought down the sails, switched on the engines and threw them into reverse. She couldn't believe it. Power boats racing in the same waters as slower craft in narrow straits where there were submerged rocks was a recipe for disaster. Her glance swept the deck. All the children were wearing life jackets as a matter of course, but some of the adults didn't swim too well, and if anyone was thrown overboard…

The power boats cut away at the last minute. They'd never had any intention of crossing her path. But for a few tense moments…

Her group thought it was the excitement of the day. And

even Ellie had to admit that the spectacle had been thrilling—
once she had realised the boats were being driven responsibly!

Only now could she accept that Alexander had been at the
helm of the lead boat. Had he really raised his hand in greeting
as he sped past, or was she imagining that? And did it matter,
since her pulse was racing all the same? She had to get over him.
But he'd really known how to drive that thing. The angle of turn
had been so acute he'd nearly stood the power boat on its end...

And now that her boat had turned into the open sea she
could see him again. Ellie blenched and tightened her grip on
the wheel. The power boats were heading straight for the
narrow channel where her father had been killed. Alexander
wouldn't know it, but he was about to race right over her
father's grave. 'No...' Ellie's voice was lost on the wind. No
one heard her. Her passengers were too interested in watching
the race to hear her, and Alexander was half a mile away.

She did what she must; she held the boat steady until in
her own mind the turgid waters had settled down again, and
the spot where she cast flowers each year was placid and
calm again. What hurt her most was the fact that Alexander
had lied to her. He had told her that nothing was settled until
everyone on the island agreed that the race should take place.
Since when had she agreed?

The truth was, he didn't need her agreement, Ellie realised.
Alexander Kosta could do exactly what he liked. He owned
the island. But he didn't own everyone on it, she thought,
firming her lips.

Ellie maintained her composure as she steered past the light-
house and entered the harbour, but she had no intention of letting
this pass. The moment her passengers were safely disembarked
she was going to find Alexander, and have it out with him.

CHAPTER TWELVE

SHE took the rickety local bus to the deep-water harbour and arrived just in time to see the magnificent power boat Alexander had been driving being winched back on board his yacht. He was supervising everything. She wasn't surprised, and it was a stroke of luck. There was no chance his burly bodyguards would allow her to board the *Olympus* unless Alexander caught sight of her first.

He spotted her immediately and waved, little guessing the tornado that was about to be unleashed.

'Alexander…'

'Ellie, what a pleasant surprise.'

As she walked up the gangway he realised something was wrong.

'Problems?'

'One or two,' she admitted, forcing a smile in case he changed his mind about letting her on board. 'Can we go somewhere to talk?'

'Of course…'

The scale of his boat in comparison to hers struck home as she walked along the deck. Ellie felt her conviction that she was right starting to drift away. Why was she here? Why was she really here? Why couldn't she just let this go? Her father would probably have been one of the first to stand and cheer when Alexander went roaring past.

Ellie's thoughts were in turmoil, but she managed to hold everything in check until they were comfortably settled in the salon. And then, when Alexander came to sit across from her, she could only see the way his hair curled around his strong, tanned face, and the whiteness of his teeth and width of his shoulders, the length of his legs…the whole package, really.

'So,' he said, snapping her out of the distraction, 'what can I do for you? Shall we start with coffee?'

It was an awkward time of day—six o'clock. He would be as keen as she was to grab a shower and change. As he snapped the intercom switch and ordered coffee for two she could smell clean denim and the sea…

'So, Ellie, what brings you here?'

'You lied to me.'

She didn't mince her words. 'About what?'

'About the races…'

'I never lie.'

'So what was that display today?'

'A trial.'

'Even a test run can cause damage—'

'And I took care to see that it wouldn't. I sought advice—'

'From whom?'

'From scientists who know this ocean as well as you do—'

'No, they don't—'

'Ellie,' he said as she sprang up.

'You could have put my boat in danger.' She kept her back to him.

'It isn't that, it's something more…isn't it?' he pressed when she didn't answer.

'Why did you have to turn down that channel?' she whispered, hugging herself.

'Because it's going to be the fastest part of the course, and I had to decide whether or not it was safe before I allowed the other drivers to use it.'

Ellie paled as Alexander's words sank in. So her father's tranquil resting place was about to become a speedway track for power-boat enthusiasts. 'You can't do that,' she said passionately, turning round.

Alexander looked at her. 'I can do what I like.'

'Without thought for other people? Yes, I see…' But she didn't, and she felt hurt; desperately hurt by Alexander's cavalier attitude and by the fact that she couldn't tell him what he'd done.

'What is it, Ellie?' he said. 'What is it you aren't telling me?'

He was growing impatient. He was drained from the flat-out racing trials, and from exercising more emotion over the past few days than he'd ever done. 'What's wrong with you?'

'What's wrong with me is you, Alexander.'

When her eyes filled with tears he reached for her. He knew he shouldn't but she looked so vulnerable, so in need of him, of being held close. Fortunately a tap at the door announcing that coffee had arrived prevented him from making any more mistakes. 'Set it down there,' he told the steward, pointing to the table between the sofas.

'Will you serve, or shall I, Ellie?' He was determined to restore an air of normality.

'I don't want coffee, Alexander,' she told him.

'Then what do you want?'

'I'm asking you…no, I'm begging you to change the course of the race.'

'Don't make such a drama of it,' he said impatiently. 'I told you I asked for advice; that is the best route for the race.'

A second passed, and then she whispered, 'Over my father's grave?'

'What?' He stared at her.

Ellie looked up at him. 'The route you took went straight over his last resting place.'

He brushed a hand over his face in disbelief, as if that could clear away the guilt inside him.

'The scientists couldn't have told you that, could they, Alexander?'

It was true; they were experts, but they weren't locals.

He let the silence hang for a moment. 'Why didn't you tell me this before?'

'Why would I?'

'If I'd had any idea—'

To his surprise she touched his arm as if to console him. She pulled it away almost immediately, as if she realised what she had done.

'You don't have to be strong all the time, Ellie. You don't have to be strong at all with me. I won't take advantage of you...ever.' Moving slowly so he didn't frighten her, he cupped her face in his hands. Brushing the tears from her cheeks with his thumb pads, he drew her closer and kissed her lightly. He stood back then and let her go. Returning to the table, he sat down and poured out the coffee as if nothing unusual had happened between them. He'd make it up to her. He'd make her father's grave a place that everyone knew and respected.

They talked for hours. The coffee went cold and Alexander was still listening. She told him about her father; she told him everything, except about the rape. In return Alexander asked her to sit on the race committee at his side. The scientists were right—her local knowledge was invaluable, he said; Ellie would help them chart the route. And then he kissed her.

She was dazed by the speed with which things happened when Alexander was in control. And when he carried her into his stateroom Ellie knew that the real miracle was that, far from dreading a man's touch, she was actually inviting it. As Alexander laid her down on the silken coverlet she reached for him. The magic whirled faster as she remembered how much pleasure he could bring her. He kissed her again, tenderly and persuasively; she wanted so much more from him now than kisses.

When Alexander deepened the kiss Ellie was ready for him, and when his stubble rasped against her neck she shivered with pleasure and pressed against him harder. Her limbs were melting as sensation throbbed throughout her body, every nerve-ending was flaring into life. Lacing her fingers through his hair, she kept him close, kissing him, rubbing her nipples against the hard muscles of his chest until he groaned with as much desire as she felt. He pushed her top up and dipped his head, capturing one tight, hot bud through the fine lace of her bra...and while he did that his other hand was teasing her neglected breast.

It was too much to endure. The sensations just grew and grew. Heat was streaming through her, making her writhe and whimper with a hunger she'd never felt before... Not even the last time, Ellie realised, because then she had half known that she wouldn't go the whole way. This time was different; this time she was his completely.

When Alexander's hand moved on to caress her belly she gasped and felt her body yearn for his touch. She was responding to some primal rhythm in her head. It dictated her actions, her thoughts, her feelings, and those were all focused on Alexander; he was the pathway to release.

He removed her clothes, stopping her from ripping them off. He calmed her down as he stripped her naked. The waiting was turning her into a seething, mindless form of heat and longing, a form that only knew Alexander must touch every part of her.

'Slow down, Ellie...'

His voice was softer than she'd heard it, and husky with desire. He left her to strip his clothes off and she missed him immediately. 'Come back to bed,' she begged; 'it's cold here without you...'

'Cold?' he said.

All right, it had never been hotter.

Ellie smiled. Alexander's glance was warm too as he kicked away his clothes. He came back, stretched out his length beside her and took hold of her.

She stared into his eyes. The expression in Alexander's was so warm and open...

He thought he knew her, Ellie realised. But he didn't know her. He didn't know the shame she felt, or that the scar on her face was only the tip of the iceberg. Seeking cover beneath the sheets, she pulled them up to her chin.

'Second thoughts?' he said, frowning.

Second thoughts...

'Ellie?'

Her heart was hammering in her chest. Alexander was stroking her, soothing her, treating her like an edgy thoroughbred who required the hands of her master to calm her down. 'No, I'm fine,' she said, pretending. 'I like it,' she told him, desperately wanting to be normal. 'Please don't stop.'

'I'm going to take things a little slower so you can enjoy them a little longer,' Alexander murmured against her mouth.

'Sounds good to me,' Ellie whispered back, sinking down again on the pillows.

He moved over her, arranging the pillows to make sure she was comfortable. Reaching up with trembling hands, she traced the contours of his face, as if to assure herself that this was no old man with leering eyes, but a young, vigorous, gorgeous man, who wanted her. She drew her fingers down over the firm swell of Alexander's lips and rasped her hand against his stubble-roughened chin, as if to reassure herself. She was confident enough to torture his hard brown nipples with her thumbnails, and to smile with pleasure hearing his sharp inhalation of breath. She was ready…she was.

There was a tense silence and then Alexander drew back sharply. 'No,' he said, 'you're not with me. Who are you with, Ellie? What's going on?'

'No one—'

'Don't lie to me—'

'I'm not—' Turning her head away, she tried to sort her thoughts out, but her mind was in turmoil.

'Why didn't you tell me, Ellie?' Alexander demanded tensely, swinging off the bed.

'Tell you what?'

'That you were a virgin?'

She could hear her elderly rapist laughing at her from the grave. She was tainted and soiled, just as he'd said she was. She was dirty and incapable of ever having a normal relationship with a man.

'You should have told me, Ellie,' Alexander said, pulling on his clothes again.

Ellie had touched his heart and found her home there, and now this. He felt betrayed. He felt he'd failed because she couldn't trust him. He wanted to protect her. He wanted her in every way a man could want a woman, Alexander realised, turning back to the bed. 'Ellie…'

Ellie had covered her ears and buried her face in the pillow. She couldn't bear to hear the tender note in Alexander's voice, or see the look in his eyes. He trusted her; he thought the best of her. He thought she was a virgin, a shrinking violent, a tender bloom, who had balked at the final hurdle, when in fact she was nothing like that. She owed him the truth. 'I'm not a virgin, Alexander.'

'What?'

The silence was unbearable.

'I'm not a virgin.'

Everything changed in that moment. Alexander's face was grim as he secured his belt. 'So, what's your game?' His eyes narrowed with suspicion. 'Do you have photographers waiting?'

'Photographers?'

'You'd better tell me, because I will find out. Are you working for some journal? Do you have a hidden camera; a tape recorder?' When she dropped her gaze and hung her head he took it as her admittance.

'Get up and get out of my bed,' he ordered harshly. 'You can use that bathroom over there—' he stabbed the air with his finger '—and when you've finished, leave the yacht and get out of my sight. I can't bear to look at you.'

Ellie tugged the sheet around her naked body. She had almost made it to the door when Alexander overtook her. 'How many men were there before me?' he demanded.

She stuttered something.

'Do you select all your marks with such care?'

Her mouth worked, but still no sound would come out.

'Come on, Ellie,' Alexander goaded her. 'It's not such a hard question to answer, is it? Is it just rich men, or is it every man you go for?'

'There's only been—'

'Yes?'

The eyes blazing into hers surely couldn't belong to the man who only minutes earlier had been caressing her with such tenderness.

'I asked you, how many?' Alexander pressed.

'One.' She flinched back as if he might hit her. The look in his eyes had that wild fury she'd seen once before.

'One,' Alexander repeated.

He drew back. He controlled his fury. He internalised his anger. He wouldn't dream of lashing out, Ellie realised. The thought of violence towards a woman was unthinkable to him. This was what she had lost.

'And was this man special to you?'

'No!' The word exploded out of her. Alexander rocked back mentally. She could see him analysing what that meant. 'He was an older man—'

'Married?'

'No! Of course not!' she protested.

'Greek?'

'No…' He seemed to relax, but every step was bringing them closer to the truth.

'A man back in England, then?'

Her silence told him the answer.

'Tell me his name.'

'I won't do that—'

'If you want to remain living on Lefkis you will.'

'Blackmail, Alexander?'

'I'm waiting for your answer.'

Sucking in a deep breath, Ellie braced herself. 'He was an old friend of my mother's—'

'An *old* friend?'

'Yes…'

The pain shot through him like a hammer blow. He couldn't believe it had happened to him twice. Just when he thought he'd put the past behind him and had a chance to find happiness with someone so very different from his first wife, his old enemy was back mocking him from the grave. He'd drawn away, thinking Ellie a virgin. Her behaviour this time and the last pointed to that. The truth she had just admitted told him she was just like his ex-wife. There was only one reason a young and beautiful woman went to bed with an old man. And, knowing that, could he ever bring himself to touch her now?

'Go, Ellie,' he said, seeing her hovering, still unsure what she should do. 'Just leave me now.' The explosion of sound came from somewhere in his guts. He turned his face away from her; he couldn't bear to look at her.

She tried to speak to him; she reached out, but by that time he was all frozen over and didn't want to know. The images in his head of Ellie pleasing an old man were so dreadful they beat any lingering tenderness out of him. All he was aware of was the blood pounding in his head. He didn't know what she did next, or what she said to him. He only knew that Demetrios Lindos's laughter was deafening as Ellie ran out of the room.

CHAPTER THIRTEEN

EVERYTHING had shriveled up inside her; even her mouth was dry, though she'd drunk a glass of freshly squeezed orange juice in one of the harbour-side cafés. Under the darkening sky that threatened rain, she was perched on the harbour wall thinking about Alexander after spending the night dozing fitfully on one of the wooden benches in the children's playground. She hadn't been able to get back to the harbour where her boat was moored at night; the local bus didn't run that late. She should have thought of that before agreeing to go on board the *Olympus*.

Maybe one day she'd get it through her head that she inhabited a different world from Alexander, Ellie reflected, gazing at his yacht. Those worlds might collide from time to time, but that was it. She had reopened old wounds and Alexander must hate her for it. He would never be able to look at her again without remembering that she had been intimate with an old man, just as the locals had told Ellie his young bride had been many years before. It had been a real eye-opener for her, and had explained a lot about Alexander's attitudes to life.

If only she could have told him the truth. But it was too late for regrets; she had to get on with her life.

Hearing the sound of winches, Ellie refocused on the

Olympus. She could see Alexander standing on the deck. His power boats were being lowered into the water, and no doubt he intended to run another trial.

She had no one to blame but herself if that trial trespassed on her father's resting place, or if it damaged the precious sea life. She had blown her opportunity to change Alexander's mind.

But not to save his life, Ellie thought anxiously, glancing at the dark, forbidding sky. If Alexander set out now he could be driving into dangers that he, as a relative newcomer to the island, couldn't know about. She could help him if he would listen to her. The locals often said that no one knew the waters around Lefkis better than she did.

It must be in the genes, Ellie thought wistfully, remembering her father. Iannis Mendoras had taught her everything she knew, and she had been an eager student. She had learned that the currents around Lefkis could be treacherous in certain weather conditions, and that when that happened boats could be driven onto the rocks...

This was like the nightmare of her father's death all over again, Ellie realised, grimacing with anxiety. It was too late to stop Alexander, as he had already secured his helmet and climbed into his boat. His men would never listen to her. But there was still a chance she could stop him reaching the most dangerous part of the course if she could reach her small inflatable in time...

As the ancient bus chugged around the harbour, Ellie tensed. This was worse than she had thought. More power boats had joined Alexander's in the choppy waters, and it looked as though the trial was turning into a full-blown race.

Ellie guessed all the drivers would want the same chance to test the route and that Alexander must have encouraged them. He was hardly the type of man who would seek an unfair advantage. But this time his principles were leading him into danger, Ellie thought, casting another anxious glance at the lowering sky. Thin rags of cloud were blowing across it, which was a bad sign. This was no short-lived squall. The sea would blow up into mountainous waves in no time, and then Alexander would have partially submerged rocks to negotiate in gale-force winds, and currents that changed course every few minutes...

She wasn't brave, or a fool, but someone had to stop Alexander killing himself.

He relished the power surging beneath him. Speed was a dangerous compulsion, but it allowed him to think of nothing else, which was exactly what he needed right now. But even when he gave the boat its head he kept thinking of Ellie. In spite of everything he was worried about her. His people had told him she hadn't returned to her boat that night. So, where was she?

At least she wouldn't be in danger on the water this time. He had given the harbour master clear instructions to warn all the owners of the local boats to stay clear of the proposed route. This was a full race trial, and to make doubly certain there would be no accidents he had ordered the course marshals to keep a look-out for anyone who was unaware of his order.

It was only borderline safe for the trial, which in his present state of mind suited him just fine, Alexander thought, glancing up at the boiling pewter clouds.

In spite of the storm clouds the water over her father's resting place had remained remarkably tranquil. But appearances could be deceptive, Ellie realised as her red inflatable slid slowly past. It was fortunate her local knowledge had allowed her to know in advance where the course marshals were likely to be located. She had evaded those in boats by waving and signalling her intention to return swiftly to harbour, and those on land by using routes they didn't even know existed.

And now all she could do was wait and block off the channel where the position of the marshals told her the power boats were meant to pass. If Alexander was as good as his word and avoided the stretch of water that meant so much to her, he'd be safe.

Cutting her engines, Ellie began to shiver with cold as the weather closed in around her. She had secured the neck of her waterproof, but the plasticised fabric offered little protection against the sudden chill in the air. It might only be late afternoon, but the sun had disappeared behind the scudding clouds and there wasn't a dry spot to be had in the tiny craft. At least it was storm-tested and almost indestructible, Ellie consoled herself. Not that she had sinking in mind, of course.

She tried a practice wave with her flag. It carried a warning symbol every sailor recognised. Divided equally into two vertical stripes of blue and yellow, the flag warned any oncoming vessel to stop immediately. She wasn't relying on that alone. She had made various stops along the way to turn guide arrows posted in the shallows towards deeper water. In all probability the power boats wouldn't even get this far but, just in case, she was ready for them.

Knuckling the spray from her eyes, Ellie peered into the gloom. She couldn't hear anything with the wind blowing in her ears. She was taking a risk, because the marshals couldn't see her. That was part of the plan, but it also left her dangerously exposed. What she meant to do was wave her flag the moment she saw the power boats coming, but in the gale-force winds she couldn't even raise her flag for more than two seconds, let alone wave it.

* * *

He had memorised the route, and was well out in front. But disappointment hit when he realised how empty his victory was going to be. This was just one more example of how money could buy everything—the best boat, the best engineers and even the best and most challenging island to race around, but it could never buy the satisfaction of winning on his own merit. If he did win the tournament, which seemed likely judging by today's performance, his victory would be hollow; just another billionaire's whim accommodated.

A woman like Ellie could have changed all that. She challenged him and made him see things differently. He had so wanted to believe she was different from the others, and when he learned that she was tainted by money too he couldn't take it. He was rapidly coming to the conclusion that money was a poison not worth pursuing.

As his anger and frustration grew Alexander opened the throttles on his boat to their fullest extent…

The power boat came out of nowhere, bearing down on her before she had time to raise her flag. She had two choices and a split-second in which to make one—she could jump overboard and try to swim out of the way of the oncoming craft, or she could stay where she was and hope the driver would see her in time.

At the same moment Alexander realised he'd lost the chasing pack he saw the red inflatable. It was stationed outside the entrance to a narrow channel. It was the channel Ellie had told him about, the channel where her father had died. He'd put it out of bounds and set the course to run at a diagonal so it missed the stretch of water that meant so much to her and took a different route.

Head down, arms braced against the wheel, he was already

committed to this new trajectory—and there would be more after him. He got a brief impression of Ellie half crouching in the shallow craft as she struggled to raise a flag. He knew it was a warning flag right away, and his heart ripped in two when he realised what she was trying to do. She was trying to save him, and he was going to kill her…

He had to turn… He had to turn now! Alexander's boat was bearing down on her like some foaming sea monster, slicing through the churning waves. Everything happened so fast after that she didn't even have time to scream. He must have seen her because his boat slewed and hit the rocks. The other boats roared past. They had seen the accident and knew the only sane thing to do was to avoid it.

Alexander's boat bounced back into the sea after defying gravity for what seemed an interminable time. Alexander was trapped beneath it…

It was a nightmare revisited, and for a moment she just froze. She was taken right back to the night when her father lost his life. She hadn't reached him in time either…

Daylight had almost gone when Ellie stripped off her waterproof. Kicking off her flip flops, she freed the lifebelt from its holding and tossed it overboard. She had to force herself to wait long enough to send up a flare. She hit the red mayday button too, before plunging into the freezing water.

It was hard to get her bearings at first. She kicked out strongly, trying to see above the towering waves. She had nothing to go on but the hulking shape of the upended boat. She dived repeatedly beneath the murky water, only to resurface and try again. The cockpit was empty; she couldn't find a trace of Alexander.

Clawing her way to the surface, Ellie gulped in air. The storm was worsening, the inflatable was drifting out of reach and she was exhausted. It took all the strength she'd got to lunge and catch hold of the lifebelt, but she was only resting for a moment, and then she would try again…

He broke the surface close to the rocks. His first thought was to turn and go back to look for Ellie. He could see the inflatable, empty and drifting free. He could see the smoke from the flare and rejoiced that she'd had the presence of mind to let one off. But where was she? Shunning the safety of the shore, Alexander plunged back into the sea.

He dived repeatedly; he refused to give up. He kept telling himself that she would survive, and that any woman who could survive him must be extraordinary. But was it enough? Was Ellie strong enough to survive this?

Her strength had almost deserted her, and what little resolve she had left was seeping away with the last of it. If only she could have told Alexander the truth. *If only,* so many times, for so many things. And now it was all too late. The old man who raped her had won after all; his triumph was complete. She was too tired to go on; too tired to save the man she loved.

She had almost given up when she heard the helicopter. As adrenalin rushed through her she began calling out, even though logic told her it would do her no good. Treading water, she waved frantically, and by some miracle the men in the helicopter spotted her…

His heart leapt when he caught sight of her through the mist and spray. He could see the pale flash of her arms as she tried to keep the water out of her face. The helicopter was overhead, and they were so close to being saved, but Ellie was hanging on to the lifebelt by her fingertips. He couldn't wait for assistance; she didn't have that long.

The thought that he might lose her drove him forward. He reached her in a matter of seconds and dragged her to him. She was almost unconscious, half-drowned and wholly incapable of doing anything to help herself. The current was pulling her one way while he kicked out the other. It was a battle of wind and rain against survival instincts, but he finally managed to bring her alongside the inflatable. Heaving her on board, he waved to let the crew in the helicopter know he'd got her...

She began coughing right away, knife pains scorching through her chest as she crouched on the floor of the inflatable. Sea water, seemingly gallons of it, poured from her mouth. But none of that mattered, because Alexander was safe. He kept his arm around her shoulders as she retched helplessly. She'd be all right now, Ellie realised, looking at him with gratitude; they'd both be all right...

The inflatable was rocking crazily as he reached up to catch hold of the rope the men had thrown down. His feet were planted wide, but even so it wasn't easy. She got up to help him catch it—typical of Ellie, always trying to help out where she could. He turned to warn her as the rope hit the deck. Too late; she had already stepped into the loop at the end of it! Seeing what had happened, the men on board the helicopter slacked off the tension. As they did so a wave caught the rope and pulled it tight again. Before he could save her she was thrown off balance and tossed into the sea.

His first impulse was to dive to save her, but if he did that he would kill her. First he had to find a knife to cut the rope.

As he wrenched the safety compartment open he prayed the broken radio was a one-off incident. He exclaimed with relief when he found what he was looking for. The knife was sharp enough for gutting fish and would make short work of the rope. Palming it, he lunged for the rope. He wasn't going to let Ellie drown in the same place as her father.

CHAPTER FOURTEEN

ELLIE woke feeling disorientated with a head full of cotton wool that felt as if it had been stamped on. It took her a while before she could work out where she was. Squinting hard through scratchy eyes, she could see white—lots of it. Bright white light, the rustle of clothes and murmuring voices, plus the unmistakable smell of disinfectant—she had to be in hospital.

She was, and she was lying on a hard, tightly sheeted hospital bed. But there was another scent reaching her now and one far nicer than the first: roses.

Slowly regaining the ability to focus properly, Ellie realised that the room was full of roses. There were several large arrangements set on tables, in what she gathered must be one of the hospital's private rooms, as well as a stack of unopened cards awaiting her attention.

Sitting up was the cue for the drum major in her head to wreak havoc. Somebody hushed her when she groaned and, too weak to fight, she sank back down on the pillows.

'Welcome back…' The nurse standing at her side smiled down at her.

'How long have I been asleep?'

'Around twenty-four hours.'

'Twenty-four hours!' Ellie regretted springing back up. 'Alexander?' she said, wincing.

'Don't worry,' the nurse soothed, easing her back down again, 'he's fine—'

'He's fine—so why isn't he here? Where is he?' Ellie said, beginning to panic. 'I want to see him—'

'I'll go and tell the doctor you're awake—'

'No! Please! Wait! I have to speak to Alexander...'

The tone of her voice made the nurse stop by the door. There was something wrong. Ellie was sure of it. It was all too good to be true—the pin-neat room and flowers, the stricken patient lying on the bed. It was like a scene from a movie—except the hero was missing. 'You said Alexander was safe...' Ellie's heart stopped beating. She'd seen those films where they lied to patients because they weren't strong enough to take the truth. 'So, where is he?'

'Kirie Kosta discharged himself yesterday,' the nurse told her. 'Don't worry—he's fine,' she reassured. 'You were lucky he was there to save you—'

Lucky? Ellie didn't imagine Alexander would see it that way. He had almost been killed because of her. She would never forgive herself and could understand if he didn't want anything more to do with her.

She discharged herself the same day. The doctor tried to persuade her to stay, insisting that her bill was paid, and it would be better for her to rest awhile...

The bill had been paid by Alexander, Ellie realised. The doctor told her he had insisted on sitting with her until they were able to assure him that she was out of danger.

'Did he mention where he was going when he left the hospital?' Ellie said offhandedly.

'To the boat?' The doctor didn't seem sure.

'Of course…' That was exactly where she expected him to go—back to the *Olympus*, where he would carry on with his life as if they'd never met. Alexander must have had his fill of hotheaded protestors who caused him nothing but trouble.

'I watched his yacht sail around the point once. Magnificent, isn't it?' The doctor turned when Ellie didn't answer, but by that time the patient had already left the room.

He listened in silence to what Kiria Theodopulos told him. He understood a lot more now. The area around Ellie's late father's resting place was to be respected and marked with a plaque. Everyone would know that this was a special place where a special man had given his own life to save that of a friend.

He left the bench in front of the harbour where the old ladies gathered each day to make their lace. '*Efharisto*…thank you, Kiria Theodopulos,' he murmured, bowing his head in respect.

'*Parakalo, Kirie Kosta,*' the old lady responded formally.

But as she made a closing gesture with her hands he noticed how her gaze slid away from him. She didn't want him staying any longer and pressing her about any other matter concerning Ellie.

Ellie's heart had started to thunder long before the rickety local bus had turned the final corner. Her boat was her home and her sanctuary, and she had never felt more relieved at the thought of getting back to it. In the past few days she had made a collection of mistakes and errors of judgement. They had almost cost Alexander his life. She needed time alone now to think her way back from all the trouble she'd caused.

Ellie had sunk into such a solemn mood that the bus driver's laughter gave her a start. Everyone on the bus had turned to stare at her. Why was that? Her cheeks flamed red. Did everyone know what she'd done?

Ellie's guilt turned to amazement when she took her first look at the harbour. There were pennants flying everywhere, and it seemed to her as though half the population of Lefkis had crowded onto the cobbled square in front of the quay. Grabbing her small bag of personal belongings, she hurried to the front of the bus.

'You're our heroine,' the bus driver explained in heavily accented English.

'I'm nothing of the sort,' Ellie disagreed.

This seemed to make no impression on the man. 'Everyone is waiting to see you, Kiria Mendoras.'

And as if this was a cue everyone on the bus started applauding.

'No, no, you're wrong,' Ellie insisted, feeling her cheeks grow red.

This had to be a misunderstanding. It was so embarrassing. She was no heroine. Ellie launched herself off the bus the moment it stopped. Racing down the quay without looking left or right, she heard the cheering, but refused to acknowledge that it was for her. If it was she was the worst type of fraud. Ellie Mendoras might be the daughter of a hero, but she was unworthy to be called by that name.

She gave a great gulp of relief when she reached her gangway. It felt so gloriously familiar beneath her feet, and now her cabin and the safety it represented was only a few steps away. She just had to go past the sturdy wooden wheel, and take the hatchway down—

'Not so fast—'

Ellie's breath shot out of her in one huge gust of disbelief. 'Alexander! Thank God you're safe!' She didn't pause to think as she threw herself at him. He was safe, and that was the only thing that mattered to her.

'Ellie…'

'Alexander,' she said more calmly, pulling away. She could just imagine what he was thinking.

'You'd better come with me; the mayor is waiting for you—'

'For me? Why?'

'You don't remember anything about the accident, do you?'

'Enough,' she murmured, avoiding his gaze. 'Why is everyone here?'

'They seem to think you're a heroine—'

'Well, that's just nonsense…'

'All right, then, but why not accept the plaudits with good grace? People have come from all over the island today—'

'But why?' She laughed self-consciously.

'Because if you hadn't stopped your little craft in the sea all the power boats would have followed me and would have been crushed against the rocks. Even the topmost scientists in the world don't share your local knowledge, Ellie. You saved those people; you saved their lives.'

'I did?'

'You did,' Alexander confirmed, 'and in recognition I'm going to ask you in front of all these people to sit on every committee concerned with the welfare of this island. I don't want another day like yesterday ever again.'

She could see he was serious. This was everything she'd wanted at the beginning of the week, but as Alexander turned away Ellie realised that the only time she would see him now was when she was sitting on one of his committees. He would share things with her, she was sure…one day there might be talk of his betrothal to some socialite, and on another maybe she'd see the ring. There was sure to be a fairy-tale wedding, and then a honeymoon in some exotic location, and after that, children…

'Ellie…Ellie?' Alexander's voice grew more insistent. 'Ellie, everyone's waiting for you to say something.'

'I'm sorry…' Ellie refocused quickly and gave a quick speech about her good feelings about the future of the island now that Alexander was at the helm.

'Very good,' he said wryly. 'I seem to have passed all the trials you set me.' As she glanced up at him, his thoughts once again turned to her protection and safety. 'I'll wrap up here,' he insisted. 'You need to rest.'

'Rest?' Ellie protested. 'I've been sleeping for a whole day.'

'Exactly,' Alexander said, matching her stare for stare.

'You don't have to fuss over me—'

'Perhaps I want to,' Alexander said.

Ellie was careful not to read anything into that. She turned away, relieved to be home, relieved to have Alexander at her side, safe and well.

Ellie's arms were full of flowers by the time the speeches had ended. There were so many smiling faces; she'd had no idea so many people cared about her. 'I'm sorry if I seemed ungrateful at first,' she said, turning to Alexander. 'It's just that this is far more than I deserve—'

'And it's not over yet,' he assured her. 'I told the mayor you'd open the dancing.'

'I'm hardly a good advertisement for Lefkis womankind,' Ellie protested, looking at her hospital fund-raiser's T-shirt, which in the absence of her ruined clothes she had been glad to tuck into someone else's patched and faded jeans.

'Leave me to be the judge of that,' Alexander suggested.

'You don't mean you're going to dance with me?'

'I'll brace myself,' he promised drily. 'Shall we?'

'Oh, if I must,' Ellie finally conceded, trying to look severe.

'Why, Ms Mendoras, I do believe you're flirting with me...'

'You're dreaming, Kirie Kosta—'

'And to think, I normally leave all that to you...'

Alexander drew Ellie close for the old-fashioned waltz, which the elders of the island had deemed appropriate to open the proceedings. They had set up a temporary dance floor on the quay, and as the music rose and fell in time with the swell of the tide Ellie relaxed a little, and gradually her worries drifted away. Dancing close to Alexander like this was magical. Even dressed in the blue jeans he'd been working in, along with the simple thonged sandals all the local men wore, he looked amazing. The scent of sunshine hung on his shirt, and the sturdy rock of confidence surrounded him. His hand had settled in the curve at the small of her back, and she felt safe.

'Are you sure you're not too tired for this?' he murmured. 'I don't want you overdoing it—'

'I'm not tired at all,' she insisted, realising it was true.

'In that case I'd better get you out of here as fast as possible...'

'Alexander? Where are you taking me?' Ellie asked as he led her away.

'Everyone will understand if we leave the party early,' he insisted.

She couldn't go there—wherever it was he intended. She was a failure in bed, and didn't need reminding about it. 'Honestly, Alexander. I'd rather stay here.'

'Well, I don't want to.'

He had saved her life, and the *Olympus* was lit up like a Christmas tree. It was hardly the right moment for seduction.

On board the *Olympus* Alexander called for champagne. 'I think we're due a small private celebration, don't you, Ellie? We'll take our drinks on deck,' he told the steward.

She relaxed. It was just as she had thought. This was a harmless invitation, and he was right, they had every cause to celebrate. Alexander was safe; what more reason did she need?

'I can't remember anything about the accident,' she admitted to him as they clinked glasses.

'That's normal,' he said. 'You saved a lot of people's lives and they won't forget. You're treading in your father's footsteps, Ellie—'

'No, I'll never do that.'

One day he'd take her and show her the plaque, but not now, not today. 'Thank you,' he said softly.

'For what?'

'For being Ellie Mendoras.' Alexander smiled.

She put her glass down.

'Shall we forget the champagne?' Alexander suggested.

'And do what?'

'Wait and see,' he said.

Ellie's fishing boat was deserted by the time they got back to it.

'Will you cast off, or shall I?' Alexander asked her.

'Don't you think I should know where we're going first?' Ellie said wryly.

'No, I don't.'

'OK, just this once, and only this once, I surrender.'

'Can I have that in writing?' Alexander flashed a look at her.

That sent her heart spinning into overdrive. Did it matter where they were going as long as they were together? Ellie thought, watching Alexander weigh anchor. There were times when the sea could give you answers that no amount of talking ever could. 'I'll take the wheel,' she said.

They had been sailing for around an hour and were heading towards one of the smaller, uninhabited islands. They worked well together, Ellie reflected. And watching Alexander work now that he had discarded his shirt and rolled up his jeans was better than any treatment she might receive in the hospital. Just seeing the way he planted his feet on the deck, or strad-dled the yard as he loosed the sails was a tonic.

And a little more than that, Ellie conceded, drawing in a ragged breath.

'We'll drop anchor soon,' he said, coming to join her at the wheel.

'Aye aye, Captain…'

'So you admit I'm in charge?' he said.

'Not a chance,' Ellie responded promptly, slapping his hand away from her wheel. 'Now, where exactly do you want me to heave to?'

'Surely you're not proposing to compromise, Ellie? I hardly know you, you've changed so much.'

'A good night's sleep makes all the difference,' she told him primly.

Alexander made no comment, but Ellie felt something stir inside her as she glanced across at him. He was happy, she realised; they both were.

CHAPTER FIFTEEN

THEY had reached the island and were moored up off shore. Alexander had elected to carry Ellie to the beach. 'So you trust me today?' he said wryly.

'I trust you every day,' Ellie admitted impulsively. Truthfully, she wasn't up for a soaking, and she wouldn't put it past Alexander to dunk her in the sea. And one thing she'd had enough of was drinking sea water.

They held an impromptu picnic on the beach, using random ingredients from her fridge and store cupboard. It was hardly a billionaire's feast, but Alexander seemed content with it. Yes, she trusted him, Ellie thought as they talked easily together. The sand was warm and soft beneath them, and the sky had cleared to a pure, crystalline blue, and she was really relaxed.

Needing sun cream, she reached for the old cloth bag she'd brought from the boat. She kept it on board with an assortment of sun lotion and other beach paraphernalia, and never cleared it out. That way it was always ready for the next trip.

The light had mellowed to soft-focus amber, washing everything in a warm, honeyed glow. It couldn't have been more romantic, Ellie thought, stealing a glance at Alexander. A *frisson* of excitement made her particularly aware, knowing, apart from their boat, creaking in the gentle swell, there was nothing and no one to disturb them.

It felt as if forever stretched before them, Ellie mused, leaning back on her hands as Alexander stared out to sea. Being away from everything had allowed him to shed the burden of being Alexander Kosta for a few hours, and that was good for him.

The view was fabulous. In front of the apron of silver sand the ocean had deepened in colour to a rich Prussian blue. As the day drew to a close and the light mellowed this provided a dramatic contrast with a silver sky that brightened to sheet gold above the horizon.

'Kiria Theodopulos hinted there was something troubling you,' Alexander murmured lazily.

Ellie was instantly alert; his laid-back attitude didn't fool her. Alexander never raised a subject without having researched it thoroughly. How much more did he know about her?

'Kiria Theodopulos is a loyal friend to you; she refused to betray a confidence however hard I pressed her—'

'You pressed her?'

Alexander turned his head. 'Well, you clam up every time I ask you anything remotely personal.'

'Don't try and turn this around and make it my fault—'

'There are things I should know.'

'Why? Why should you know, Alexander?' Ellie said, sitting up.

'Because I need to understand you,' he said, refusing to break the mood as she had. 'That's essential if we're going to be working together, don't you think?'

'Are you asking my opinion, Alexander?' She was prickling all over, while Alexander just lay there, completely relaxed. 'No, I didn't think so.'

'I will get to the bottom of it…'

Ellie had seen that deceptively slumberous look before, and knew that Alexander could be like a dog with a bone when he had to. 'Hummus?' she suggested, determined to change the subject. 'I thought it might make a nice starter—'

'I'd rather start with the truth…'

Tension had set in across her shoulders, but she was going to try and keep this pleasant. She hadn't realised Alexander had brought her here to lower her guard and quiz her; she should have known better, Ellie realised as she reached for the chilled Pinot Grigio and two glasses. 'Will you open the wine, or shall I?'

'Give,' Alexander murmured in the same lazy tone, reaching out his hand.

The atmosphere lightened as they ate; their simple lunch was delicious. Ellie was just beginning to think she had been over-reacting when a freak wave caught them unawares. She was still laughing as she got to her feet. 'I hope that's the last soaking I have for a while!' she exclaimed, brushing herself down.

From sprawling on the sand as if he never wanted to get up, Alexander had reacted like lightning to retrieve the contents of her old cloth bag.

'What's this?'

Ellie's stomach took a dive when she saw what Alexander was holding out to her.

'I asked you a question,' he said in an ominously low voice. 'Why do you carry a pepper spray in your bag? Don't you trust me?' he pressed when she didn't speak.

'Of course I do—'

'It doesn't look that way to me.'

'Alexander, please—'

'The only reason any woman carries one of these is if she thinks she's at risk of attack. Well? Are you going to explain?'

'It's been in my bag forever—'

'Since when, exactly?'

'Alexander—'

'Don't press me? Is that what you're telling me, Ellie? Why shouldn't I press you? What are you hiding from me?' Dropping the canister into her bag, Alexander dumped it at her feet.

She'd had it since the rape.

'Are you going to tell me?' Hands on hips, he stood confronting her. 'Seems to me this isn't something you can just brush under the table.'

'I don't want to brush anything under the table.'

'Then tell me what this is about.'

'Please don't make me do this, Alexander.'

'So you can hide forever?' He threw his arms wide in exasperation. 'I can't make you do anything you don't want to, Ellie; whether you should is another matter.'

She paused, then in a soft whisper began to admit the truth. 'I haven't been entirely honest with you—'

'I think I've managed to work out that much for myself.'

'Don't—'

'Don't what? Don't bracket you with my wife?'

She stared at him, ashen-faced. 'I'm not like your wife.' Ellie shook her head, distressed. 'I'm nothing like her—'

'You sold your soul to an old, rich man.'

There, the words were out; he couldn't help himself. Would the bitterness never leave him? Would Demetrios Lindos always win? He watched her hug herself and turn away, and he felt bad. He was allowing himself to be dragged down by something a man had done years ago, and punishing Ellie into the bargain. 'I want to help you,' he said, 'but you won't let me.'

'I don't need your help,' she said, wrapping her arms around her waist, 'I never have.'

'I know how hard things have been for you—'

'Is this the part where you offer me money?' she said, turning around; she looked so hurt.

'Money?' Truthfully, that had never occurred to him.

'Some sort of *special* fee for when I sit on one of your committees?'

She said it in a way that made him think she must imagine he had intended setting her up as his mistress, and that talk of the work she would do on the committees was just an excuse, a cover. 'I was going to try and work out some form of payment. There's nothing wrong with that. Your local knowledge is invaluable. I know things can't be easy for you—particularly when the tourist season comes to an end.'

Did Alexander have any idea how patronising that sounded? Ellie hoped not. She didn't need his money. She had always managed somehow. She had her pride just as he had his, and now her anger was rising on a swift upward trajectory. 'You accuse me of being like your wife and then you offer me money—don't you find that just a tad ironic?'

'Don't be so defensive. If you don't want my help—'

'Frankly, Alexander, I don't,' she told him.

Ellie was angry with herself. It seemed no matter how many times her silly little dreams were shattered Alexander could find another piece of her stupid fantasy to stamp on—her fault for falling for a billionaire; she had no sense of proportion sometimes. When Alexander had first mentioned sitting on a committee with him she had been thrilled, not least because that meant seeing more of him, but now she saw he had only been offering her a handout like a prince to a beggar.

And pride wasn't confined to billionaires, she thought, staring him in the face. 'Whatever you think, *I* can't be bought—'

'The old man that did that to your face might disagree...'

The blood drained from her face. She should have remembered that Alexander always played to win. 'Who told you that?' she managed.

'There are others on this island with fewer principles than Kiria Theodopulos; you would do well to remember that, Ellie.'

'You think I don't know that,' she said, fighting back.

'Remind me,' Alexander pressed on cruelly, his face completely transformed. 'What was your excuse for sleeping with that man? Was it "he likes me to read to him"? Or did he find it hard to sleep unless you had your little chat first?'

Ellie was on the point of wiping the contempt off Alexander's face with an angry slap when she realised he was replaying what had happened to him. His hurt cut deep; the sense of betrayal had never left him. It might have propelled him like a meteorite through the business world, but inside, emotionally, he was still in that same place he'd been all those years ago, when his young bride had left him on their wedding day.

Thankfully, Alexander wasn't the only one who had confidants amongst the local population; there wasn't much she didn't know about him. 'I never slept with the man who did this to me—'

'You said you did!' he exclaimed. 'How can you lie to me now?'

'Because it's true,' Ellie insisted, holding his gaze. 'I told you I wasn't a virgin, and I'm not. I told you I had sex with an old man. But I never said I slept with him—'

'And I'm supposed to feel better now? Where did you have sex? In his study? On the floor? Or was it over his desk?'

'Alexander!' Ellie bit back, stopping him in his tracks. 'It was in his study…' But as she remembered her righteous indignation dropped away.

'In his study,' Alexander said contemptuously.

'It was sex—'

'And did he pay you?'

'Of course not!'

'So he snapped his fingers, and you went running—'

'It wasn't like that—'

'Then how was it?' Alexander roared at her, his face full of anger and contempt.

'I can't give you the answers you need to make the past go away—'

'Make the past go away?' he said incredulously. 'Why would I want the past to go away when I owe everything I am to those years?'

Because it's destroying you, Ellie thought, determined to have her say. 'I can't tell you why you lost your bride to Demetrios Lindos. I can only tell you what happened to me—'

'Money,' he cut across her. 'That's what happened to you— that's why you're here now. There's no mystery there. I thought better of you, Ellie—'

'Don't mistake me for your wife—'

'Then tell me what happened. Make me understand…'

'It was sex.' It wasn't enough; she could see that. 'He raped me, Alexander!' She yelled it at him, and when the sound waves died away they stood staring at each other, unmoving.

'What did you say?'

'He sent for me,' Ellie explained haltingly. 'He said he wanted to talk to me about a monument for my father. I trusted him. I've never told anyone before…' Her eyes glistened with unshed tears.

'Go on,' Alexander urged gently.

'I can't tell you any more, because I blacked out. I only know that what happened to me was the most horrible thing ever…'

'Ellie…' He didn't say any more, he didn't need to, he just put his arm around her shoulders and led her to a place where they could sit overlooking the sea.

They sat listening to the ocean rolling back and forth; timeless, endless…side by side; close, but not touching, until Ellie said, 'We'd talked about the monument, and I was just about to leave, when…'

He didn't prompt her. He was afraid that if he did she would clam up again, and more than him needing to know, it was important that she let the evil out.

'He'd been so kind to me…' She looked at him in bewilderment, as if she still couldn't quite believe what had happened to her. 'I thought he was so generous suggesting a memorial for my father I didn't suspect…'

She spoke quickly, telling him everything she remembered as if she had to get it over with, and there was a time limit to her statement that she mustn't overstep. He couldn't even begin to imagine what she'd been through, and what hurt him most was that all he could do now for her was listen.

'I expected him to call a servant to show me out when our meeting ended, but instead he got up from his chair. And then I thought he'd tripped when he got close to me, and grabbed me, and so I reached out to help him…'

That was so typical of her, Alexander thought grimly. She would always think the best of everyone.

'Now I realise that he must have lunged,' she said, shaking her head in disbelief as if she still couldn't believe she hadn't seen it coming.

Her naïvety was one of her sweetest characteristics, but it could also be a threat to her safety. 'Ellie…'

'I tried to save him…' She started laughing, but it was a sad sound. 'He knocked me back on the couch and held me

down. I'd worn a skirt to go to the big house, because I wanted
to look nice in honour of my father's memory. The cigar was
in his hand, and I was trying to avoid it…avoid him; his hands
were all over me. I couldn't breathe, I couldn't move…
couldn't stop him, Alexander—'

But he stopped her there, putting his arms around her and
drawing her close. But she couldn't look at him, she still
thought she was to blame. He wanted to rage at heaven for
allowing her to believe such a travesty.

'When he'd finished,' she muttered against his chest, 'I was
hysterical. I couldn't believe what had happened; what he'd
done. He grew angry then, and told me to shut up. He said I
should be grateful…I should have enjoyed it…I should feel
honoured that he'd been the one to take my virginity. And when
I wouldn't stop crying he stubbed out his cigar on my cheek.'

She had been so matter-of-fact about it he wanted to cry
for her. Holding her in his arms and murmuring to her was
like comforting a wounded child. But he didn't want Ellie as
a kid sister; he wanted a lot more than that.

'No man will ever want me,' she said in the same frank tone.
'That's right, isn't it, Alexander? What he said to me is true—'

'No!' he exclaimed. Drawing her hand down from her
cheek, where she was already tracing the scar, he said, 'That's
nothing but a blemish that can be repaired. It's what's inside
you that counts, and it's what's inside you that I love…'

She stared at him as if she still didn't understand what he
was saying.

'I love you, Ellie,' he said, dipping his head so he could
stare her in the eyes. 'I'm nothing without you. And I'll wait
for you as long as it takes…'

'Alexander…I love you too.'

They stared at each other for a moment, and then, cupping

Ellie's tear-stained face in his hands, he kissed her very gently on the mouth. It would be a long road back, but he would wait for her forever, if forever was how long it took.

CHAPTER SIXTEEN

It was a full six months later before the wedding.

Two sides of the same coin, Ellie and Alexander had both come to accept that what they really needed to make their day special was tinsel and lights and glitz and sparkle. Where better than a capital city at Christmas? They chose London. Ellie's magical Christmas wedding was going to be held in one of the top hotels…

Every day of that six months Alexander had courted Ellie with old-fashioned propriety under the watchful gaze of Kiria Theodopulos. Ellie thought their courtship should make the record books as the longest stretch of enforced chastity that any bride-to-be had been forced to endure, and was totally on edge as Kiria Theodopulos helped her put on her wedding dress.

Sexual frustration was a terrible thing, Ellie thought, jumping every time anyone came near her. She could only think of one thing: Alexander. He had grown even more gorgeous, and a great deal more provocative as the wedding grew closer. He took the greatest pleasure in teasing her, but every time she thought they would manage to evade Kiria Theodopulos and indulge in some seriously time-consuming premarital investigations, he handed her back again.

But at least she'd got the wedding dress right, Ellie

thought hopefully, turning to see her back view. In line with Alexander's determination that she must have a change from oil-stained dungarees she had gone all out with a fairy-tale gown. Sprinkled with tiny jewels that danced in the light, it cinched her waist and fell in billows of winter-white chiffon to the floor. It had a long train and to keep her warm there was a velvet cape to wear over the top of it. The flip flops had been left behind, and on her feet she was wearing dainty jewelled shoes. She would walk the few steps to the tiny chapel next door along a red carpet provided for the occasion by the hotel.

She felt exactly like Cinderella. Well, except for the scar on her cheek, Ellie thought, trying to be patient as the couturier and Kiria Theodopulos fussed over her. But it didn't matter any more; it was just a mark. Alexander had offered to pay for the best plastic surgeon if that was what she wanted, but she had told him that she would wait for her first face lift and then ask for a quantity discount.

Alexander had been right about so many things, not least of which was the fact that they had both taken themselves too seriously in the past. Over the past six months they had learned to relax and laugh, and together they had found a way to put the past behind them. There was one exception, and that was the memorial Alexander had erected at the entrance to the channel where her father had been killed. The inscription read 'To all brave seamen who have lost their lives in dangerous waters', but the statue had the face of Iannis Mendoras.

'There!' the couturier exclaimed, standing back to admire his handiwork. 'What do you think?' he added, clasping his hands with concern.

What did she think? It was very different from her usual look. The gown more than made up for years of wearing work clothes. She looked voluptuous, and with her auburn hair spilling round her shoulders she looked almost beautiful.

Would Alexander approve? Ellie went hot and cold. He might think she had gone over the top. He might not. He might throw her on the bed and ravish her on the spot—she certainly hoped so.

She was sure he had enjoyed subjecting her to a prolonged period of chastity. She couldn't remember now when she'd passed from dreading sex to being obsessed by it every waking moment. But she was…obsessed by it. And now she could only hope that the wedding ceremony, romantic as it was, would be fast—and the reception even faster.

As she took hold of her bouquet of red roses the emerald cut diamond on Ellie's wedding finger flashed fire, reminding her of something Alexander had said to her. He'd said they must have something wonderful to look back on as well as something wonderful to look forward to, and that he would make sure of it. He had insisted that the start of the process must include a fabulous ring.

Ellie smiled, remembering her naïvety when Alexander had handed her the cut-crystal casket. It had contained what she imagined was a pebble. She'd hardly been able to hide her disappointment, and had barely managed a husky, 'Very nice…' At least she'd remembered her manners and had thanked him, while wondering what on earth she was going to do with his gift.

'I suggest you have it cut and polished,' he said, deadpan, 'and then I think you'll find it makes a very nice diamond ring…'

Only Alexander would think of giving her an unpolished diamond as an engagement present. His love of teasing her knew no bounds…

Dangerous thoughts! Ellie warned herself, grimacing. If she concentrated on the many ways Alexander liked to tease she wouldn't make it to the wedding. But his gift had been special and unique. She hoped he would feel the same about her wedding gift to him when she handed him the ownership documents for her fishing boat. It was all she had to give him, and it was her most precious possession, but she'd seen his face when he'd sailed it, and she hadn't seen that look since the last time she'd seen her father at the helm.

'*Pame?* Ready?' Kiria Theodopulos asked Ellie in heavily accented English. 'We should go now…'

With a traditional black headscarf to cover her silver hair the old lady was wearing a bright traditional dress consisting of a beautifully embroidered floor-length skirt and a matching jacket in heavy red velvet. Her white blouse was intricately decorated with lace, and over the skirt there was an apron stitched in black and gold.

'You look beautiful,' Ellie told her, smiling.

'And so do you,' her old friend said, clasping Ellie's hands.

Alexander insisted on carrying her over the threshold of the Presidential suite. 'It's only for one night,' he explained, as if that were a burden she must somehow endure. 'And then we'll be flying out to meet the *Olympus* in Lefkis, and you can go anywhere in the world.'

'As long as I'm with you we can stay in dock for all I care…'

'It isn't like you to be so easily pleased,' Alexander observed drily. 'Should I be suspicious?' he demanded, lowering his new bride to her feet.

'You can't let me go yet. It's far too soon…'

'And why is that?' Alexander murmured, drawing her close.

'Because we're not in the bedroom yet…'

'I thought we'd have champagne… Ah, well, some people are never satisfied,' he said, sweeping her off her feet.

Ellie shrieked with excitement as Alexander carried her across the room. Kicking open the bedroom door, he strode across the magnificent room and set her down on the bed. 'Would you like me to help you undress?'

'You'd better—'

'Shall I start with your shoes?'

'As long as you don't stop there…'

'For this one evening your smallest wish is my command—'

'In that case I'd better take advantage,' Ellie said pragmatically. Leaning back on her hands, she extended one dainty jewelled foot. Alexander looked amazing, kneeling there; she could hardly believe it had come to this. The formal dress suit only emphasised his rugged maleness.

He tossed her shoes aside and then removed his jacket.

'Aren't you going to take your shirt off?'

'Patience…first your stockings,' he insisted.

Ah, more teasing—tit for tat. She shuddered with desire as he reached up to detach her stockings from the suspenders. So close, and yet so far…

He took his shirt off.

Ellie sighed with frustration. She could hardly breathe for excitement.

'Now you're seeing the benefits of restraint—'

'Am I?'

'You soon will,' Alexander promised with a wicked smile.

'Just don't take too long,' Ellie said breathlessly as he turned her to undo all the tiny buttons at the back of her dress. 'Can't we just rip it off?'

'And spoil the couturier's handiwork? No,' Alexander said, taking his time to free each small pearl.

When she was down to petticoats and bra he loosened his belt.

Ellie gasped as Alexander began kneading her feet. He made her lie down on the pillows so she could enjoy the tiny shock waves spinning through her. He moved on to her legs and made her groan, but there was still a froth of petticoats to negotiate, and he showed no sign of going there.

'Alexander, if you don't stop teasing me…'

'Would you rather relax? I could take a walk—'

'No, you couldn't!' Ellie assured him, grabbing hold of him to make sure. 'You're not going to disappoint me now—'

'I sincerely hope not,' he agreed.

By this time she was trembling uncontrollably.

'Are you cold?' he said drily.

'Cold? No.' She was on fire, which Alexander very well knew.

He slipped the straps of her petticoat from her shoulders, exposing the full swell of her breasts in the flimsy lace bra.

'Alexander…' His name came out on a sigh of complaint. Apart from the bra and her gossamer-fine briefs she was naked. How could he make her wait like this?

He smiled. He knew the torment she was going through.

Kneeling, he kissed her belly and cupped her hips in his big, strong hands. But before she had chance to properly enjoy what he was doing he started freeing the catch on his trousers—

'Let me…' She put her hands over his. She could feel his warmth, his power, and sense the energy at her disposal. She took her time opening the buttons as he had, and then even more time pushing the fabric over his lean, hard hips.

'Patience,' he said when she gasped.

'No, no more patience,' she argued breathlessly. 'I've waited long enough…'

She pressed against him skin to skin, heart to heart, breathing in unison, fast and strong. She rubbed herself against him shamelessly, urgently. 'I can't wait any longer, Alexander. You can't make me wait...'

Bringing her beneath him...he kissed her hard, holding her firmly the way she wanted him to. Moving down the bed, he claimed her neck, then her breasts, suckling each one before tugging cruelly at her nipples through the fine gossamer lace.

She didn't wait for permission before freeing the catch and casting her bra aside. She'd had enough of clothes separating them now. But when she tried to pull her briefs off Alexander stopped her.

'I make the rules, and I set the pace...'

'If you insist,' Ellie agreed, moving sinuously beneath him.

'Witch!'

'Isn't it time I teased you?' she said, feeling him hard and huge, thrusting against her.

'Just this once,' Alexander groaned in agreement, but as he spoke he removed her tiny briefs.

Before she knew it her legs had slipped over his shoulders and he was tasting her...licking her and sucking until sensation burst inside her.

'You're very greedy,' he observed.

'I love it when you're stern with me,' Ellie purred, arching her back as Alexander started stroking her buttocks. 'Couldn't you...?'

'No,' he murmured against her mouth, 'you must wait.'

'I don't want to wait...' But this wasn't so bad, Ellie conceded as Alexander dropped kisses on her trembling buttocks. He paid particular attention to the tops of her thighs, but didn't linger nearly long enough before moving on until he reached the backs of her knees. She gasped and hugged the pillow. 'I don't think I can bear this...'

'Force yourself,' Alexander suggested drily.

'All right, I will,' Ellie agreed, determined to brave it out. She couldn't believe how sensitive she had become. There wasn't a single part of her that wasn't singing to Alexander's tune now. Just as he had been planning for the past six months. 'You've turned me into a sex addict,' she complained.

'Lucky for you, I know a cure for that…'

'You do?' She sighed happily.

When he turned her on her back she knew she had to have him. No more waiting. No more delays. Now!

During the wedding ceremony Alexander had promised to worship her with his body, and she had every intention of making him live up to that promise, starting now.

He was so gorgeous. She feasted her eyes on him. He made her feel very small, tiny, and extremely needy where a variety of pleasures were concerned. Alexander's shoulders were massive as he loomed over her, and his biceps with his arms flexed were like iron. Those pectoral muscles felt delicious when he rubbed his chest against her…

She was moist and swollen, and desperate for release, and parted her legs to let him move between her thighs. 'No more teasing, Alexander.' It was both a question and a command. Her fingers bit into firm, tanned flesh, and her mouth connected greedily with hot, hard skin, and then she gasped, having reached down and found something it took two hands to encompass…something warm and hard that pulsed in her grip and made her need him more than ever. 'I want you,' she insisted hoarsely.

'And I can deny you nothing,' Alexander murmured with amusement.

He brushed back and forth, very lightly, allowing her just a taste of sensation. She had to beg and gasp before he would allow her the tip, and then he only teased her by withdrawing again.

The sensation was like nothing she had ever felt before...*nothing*. It made a nonsense of the past and all the nightmares, though he was so big she drew a sharp breath as he moved deeper.

'Am I hurting you?'

'Absolutely not,' Ellie insisted. If he stopped now she'd go mad.

Alexander took her slowly, aware of his great size. He filled her completely, stretching and massaging until every frantic, frustrated fantasy was fulfilled ten times over.

'Is that good?' he said, as if he didn't know.

'Don't stop.' Ellie managed to gasp out the order between groans. She was moving with him, responding to the rhythm, gripping his buttocks and urging him on, drawing her knees back and digging her fingers into his shoulders as she commanded him to move faster, to move harder, and never, never to stop.

Alexander brought her to the edge again and again. He watched her tumble off with more satisfaction than she knew, until finally she fell asleep in his arms.

She had either blacked out from extremes of pleasure, or exhaustion, Ellie decided when she woke later. She was safe in Alexander's arms, and he was kissing her. 'I wouldn't have believed that possible,' she said.

'Well, you certainly seem to have got the knack of it,' Alexander observed drily, dropping kisses on her neck.

'I'm being serious,' she whispered. 'Until I met you I'd given up all hope of having a normal life.'

His lips pressed down wryly. 'It will hardly be normal with me...'

'I'm talking about love, family, babies...'

'One thing at a time...'

'How do you mean?'

'Love…' He kissed her. 'Family…' He brought her hand with the glittering wedding band to his lips and kissed it. 'Babies…'

Ellie groaned as Alexander took her again. She'd had no idea such pleasure was possible.

'You don't know what you've done for me,' Alexander told her some time later.

'I've allowed you to look forward to a future full of challenge?' Ellie suggested mischievously.

Taking hold of her hand, Alexander smiled agreement and kissed her palm. 'I wouldn't have it any other way,' he insisted. 'Oh, and I almost forgot…'

'What?' Ellie said as he reached beneath the bed.

'I have a gift for you from one of the young girls on Lefkis. She said to wish you a happy Christmas.'

'For me?' Ellie said in bemusement as Alexander handed her the small package. 'What is it?'

'I have no idea. Why don't you open it and see?'

When Ellie opened the small, carefully wrapped gift she exclaimed with pleasure. 'My mother's gold chain… She returned it to me, Alexander. But why—?'

He cut her off with a kiss. 'Maybe because she wants you to be as happy as I do, Ellie. Happy Christmas, my darling…'

'More presents?' Ellie stared at the envelope Alexander was holding out to her.

'Well, go on, open it,' he said.

Ellie's eyes widened. 'You're giving me an island?'

'Half an island. You'll share the responsibilities of Lefkis with me. Don't you want it?'

'I—er—it's just that…' Ellie was completely stunned by the extent of Alexander's generosity, as well as his trust in her; they'd both come such a long way.

'You'll be able to sit on every committee now,' he pointed out. 'Well? What do you think?'

'Are you serious?'

'I've never been more serious in my life. At least you'll have a voice.' He began to smile.

'Will I have time for all this?' Ellie murmured, already making plans.

Removing the letter from her hand, Alexander drew her down the bed again. 'Not too much time,' he promised drily, 'but enough…'

'In that case,' Ellie gasped, 'I accept…'

LAYING DOWN THE LAW
by Susan Stephens

Sheltered and naïve Carly Tate is out of her depth. Dark, dangerous Lorenzo Domenico isn't only her mentor and tutor, he's also the first man to make her heart race. But she knows the gorgeous Italian will never see past her frumpy clothes and embarrassing innocence. Little does she realise that, to Lorenzo, Carly is a breath of fresh air…

HIS MISTRESS, HIS TERMS
by Trish Wylie

Rich, gorgeous playboy Alex Fitzgerald has his sights set on Merrow O'Connell. Initially he needs her interior design skills, but soon they're on different terms – she's perfect mistress material! Merrow has learned not to let anyone close and is determined to stay single – so what will she do when the billionaire playboy wants her to be *more* than just his mistress…?

MILLS & BOON

MEDICAL™

Proudly presents

Brides of Penhally Bay

*A pulse-raising collection of emotional,
tempting romances and heart-warming stories by
bestselling Mills & Boon Medical™ authors.*

January 2008
The Italian's New-Year Marriage Wish
by Sarah Morgan

Enjoy some much-needed winter warmth with
gorgeous Italian doctor Marcus Avanti.

February 2008
The Doctor's Bride By Sunrise
by Josie Metcalfe

Then join Adam and Maggie on a 24-hour rescue mission
where romance begins to blossom as the sun starts to set.

March 2008
The Surgeon's Fatherhood Surprise
by Jennifer Taylor

Single dad Jack Tremayne finds a mother for his
little boy – and a bride for himself.

*Let us whisk you away to an idyllic Cornish town –
a place where hearts are made whole*

COLLECT ALL 12 BOOKS!

*Available at WHSmith, Tesco, ASDA, and all good bookshops
www.millsandboon.co.uk*

MILLS & BOON
100 YEARS
of pure reading pleasure

100 Reasons to Celebrate

2008 is a very special year as we celebrate Mills and Boon's Centenary.

Each month throughout the year there will be something new and exciting to mark the centenary, so watch for your favourite authors, captivating new stories, special limited edition collections…and more!

www.millsandboon.co.uk

FREE!

4 Books
and a surprise gift!

We would like to take this opportunity to thank you for reading this Mills & Boon® book by offering you the chance to take FOUR more specially selected titles from the Modern™ series absolutely FREE! We're also making this offer to introduce you to the benefits of the Mills & Boon® Reader Service™—

- ★ **FREE home delivery**
- ★ **FREE gifts and competitions**
- ★ **FREE monthly Newsletter**
- ★ **Exclusive Reader Service offers**
- ★ **Books available before they're in the shops**

Accepting these FREE books and gift places you under no obligation to buy, you may cancel at any time, even after receiving your free shipment. Simply complete your details below and return the entire page to the address below. You don't even need a stamp!

YES! Please send me 4 free Modern books and a surprise gift. I understand that unless you hear from me, I will receive 6 superb new titles every month for just £2.89 each, postage and packing free. I am under no obligation to purchase any books and may cancel my subscription at any time. The free books and gift will be mine to keep in any case.

P7ZEF

Ms/Mrs/Miss/Mr ....Initials ....

Surname .... **BLOCK CAPITALS PLEASE**

Address ....

....

....Postcode ....

Send this whole page to:
UK: FREEPOST CN81, Croydon, CR9 3WZ